gold is not even valuable enough. To Sherene Holly Cain, you have a gift for the written word that is not lost on me. I see your talent and growth in everything that you write. Never give up on your dream because your type of writing is needed and appreciated. To everyone that has taken this journey with me either as a passenger or sometimes helping me drive; I appreciate all of you.

# DEDICATION

No matter how many books you have written I think that all authors doubt themselves a little. Did I make this story as good as the last? Will my readers understand what I am trying to say? Is this worth writing about? An author that is not strong may succumb to the temptation to quit. Never mind the readers that support you, never mind the fact that you love this, never mind that you wake up with a story in your heart. I almost gave up many times along this perilous journey, but an angel came in the form of a woman with admirable beauty and remarkable strength. Shemethia Bryant, God made no mistake by

# ACKNOWLEDGMENTS

The first thanks always goes to my father in Heaven who has closed doors no man can open and opened doors no man can close. I thank all of my Write House Family you all know who you are. A special thanks goes out to Cole Hart and Torica Tymes who always lend a listening ear and give sound advice. To all of the many authors I count as friends and family, I thank you so much. The late-night texts and phone calls help to keep me encouraged in times when I don't know where a story is going. To all of my readers, I cannot thank you enough for staying on me about characters, giving me suggestions, and even enquiring into how I am feeling in my personal life. To my business partner, LaQuita Cameron, the world could never really know how sweet you are. Besides being outwardly gorgeous you are also beautiful inside. You have a heart of platinum because placing you in my path at this moment. I didn't remember you from back in the day, so it was like meeting you for the first time, but that kinship was already there. You have been there not only reading everything I have written but also advising me on what needed work. Your opinion has always been not only invaluable but also needed and respected. You and Christopher Bryant have welcomed me and my husband into your lives as if we were always there and we do not often receive that. I thank you very much for that and I hope we have returned the love. I love you and cannot say enough how much you mean to me. Thank you from the bottom of my heart.

# A HOOD LOVE

# IN ATLANTA 4

**By: Mz. Demeanor**

# Table of Contents

# CHAPTER 1

MARISSA

Tay continued to mug me as he talked on the phone. I looked again at this high-yellow baby in disbelief. There was absolutely no way that he could be the father with him being the color of milk chocolate and myself an Oreo. I wanted to just take that baby back to the nursery and ask for a darker version just to shut him up. *Damn who was I with last?* A vivid picture of four different guys came to mind. I surely hoped it was none of them because they were all trifling and one of them was a close friend of Todd's.

I looked up in time to see Tay hanging up the phone. He ran his hands over his head before standing to his feet.

"I'ma step out for a minute. I think your peoples on their way up here." Before I could say anything, he had slipped out of the door. I felt like crying, but that required energy that I didn't even have yet. This was some straight up bullshit. I had let my life go from zero to a hundred ever since I set foot in Atlanta. Memories of my first day here flooded my mind as I began to feel the effects of my pain meds.

"Girl, get your fast ass in the house while you out here tryin' to pose." Daddy stormed past me carrying a few boxes stacked on top of each other.

Leave it to him to try to embarrass me in front of the sexy new neighbor Mona had just introduced her half-breed lookin' ass to. She did the same damn thing when we were in Louisville; always using green eyes, curly hair, and light skin to get whoever she wanted. Never mind she didn't really have too much booty and her breasts were smaller, even with her being older than me. I was tall, dark and lovely with a flat stomach and an ass you only saw on TV.

Daddy walked back out, shooting me a warning look, so I made sure to bend over in my yoga pants and pick up a heavy umbrella stand. I saw him look over Mona's shoulder as I switched by, giving him an eye full. She was talking his head off and hadn't even paid attention to him licking his lips.

I placed the umbrella stand in the living room and stopped to admire him from the front door.

"That girl has no taste. What the hell would she want with that black ass ape anyway?" Mama remarked, sliding past me with a box of her makeup.

I just turned up my nose to her color-struck ass. I saw a tall, dark and handsome chocolate drop whose bald head glistened under the sun shining like new money.

"If you don't pick up a box, I'll..."

I didn't let Daddy finish his sentence because I knew he would make good on any threat coming from his mouth. Instead, I marched outside and grabbed a box that was labeled Tools. Not thinking it would be too heavy, I yanked it up and heard a terrible snapping sound. The pain that shot down my back caused me to drop the box onto the grass.

Todd ran past Mona to help me as she stood there pretending to be concerned. She didn't look too happy when he helped me over to the porch to sit down, though. I knew from that day that he would be easy to get.

I was relieved when the phone rang, bringing me out of my memories. There was no way that Todd should be on my mind at a time like this.

"Hello," I answered dryly.

"How are you feeling, baby?" Mama asked.

"I feel horrible, to be honest."

"Well, you should feel horrible, being that you are too young to be someone's mama. You did good with this one though, she has a beautiful complexion like her granny."

I immediately regretted asking Tay to send her a picture of the baby because I knew she would say something ignorant at some point, and, as usual, she didn't disappoint.

"Ma, could you please not start that? I really don't need to hear that right now."

"Well, it's the truth. What did you name her anyway?"

I sighed, knowing that she was about to have a fit. "We named her Tavonda."

I could only imagine the faces Mama was giving me at that moment, and the thought of pissing her off actually made me laugh.

"Ugh. I at least hope that she took the Middleton last name then."

"Why? He ain't my damn daddy. My daddy is in prison getting bent over right about now," I quipped.

"Look here, you are not too old to get the hell slapped out of you. You watch your mouth. Jason may have been a little hard on you, but he did more than Ivory ever thought about doing. Ivory has been getting down with the get down for years, so I don't really have nothing to say about that."

I was disgusted that she'd dealt with a man that she knew was messing with other men. I wish Tay would try me like that.

"I gave her Tay's last name because we will be getting married eventually."

She sucked her teeth, and I imagined that she was also biting her nails like she always did when she got nervous. At that moment, I heard the clacking of footsteps. My door popped open and Mona stood there with gifts and flowers.

"Mama, let me call you back."

# CHAPTER 2

MONA-LISA

"She is just perfect, "I cooed snuggling up with Tavonda. She looked so tiny in Delano's hands.

"She is beautiful," he whispered in awe.

I silently prayed that our children looked half as beautiful as this one. Her hair was covered in rows of soft curls long enough to braid and her dimples overtook her face. She looked nothing at all like Tay, just like he said. Speaking of which, we had been here over 30 minutes and had yet to see him.

Marissa was too busy texting to pay any attention to us. She looked a mess with her hair all over the place and her nose had spread considerably, but she hadn't gained much weight at all. I, on the other hand, felt like the Good Year blimp.

"Girl, Facebook is goin' crazy over my baby. I put her pic up an hour ago and got three hundred likes already."

I looked up at Delano annoyed, but he just shrugged. I felt like it was a little disrespectful for her to be posting pics without asking Tay how he felt about it. It was bad enough he would have to explain why his baby didn't look like him.

"Are you going to open your stuff?" I asked. I had spent too much time and money putting together the perfect gifts for her and she didn't even have the decency to open them.

"You sat them on the floor like I was gon' be able to reach them. I mean, damn, I did just have a baby," she asserted nastily.

To avoid confrontation, I just ignored her smart-ass statement.

"Baby, can you please hand her those bags?"

Del handed Tavonda to me and walked across the room to retrieve the packages. Inside there were all sorts of cute picture frames, a birth pillow, baby journal, and mini camcorder, not to mention several outfits

"Damn, you must have spent a lil change on this stuff. Thank you."

"I'm glad you like it. I got your room set up with some stuff at home so you will have everything you need." The mention of *her room* made Del's jaw clench. Although he had agreed to let her and Tay stay with us, he was still not overly fond of the idea.

"I'm about to go see if I can find Tay," he mouthed and exited the room.

I shook my head before glancing over at Marissa who was all into her phone once again.

"You just gonna sit on Facebook all day or are you gonna tell me who this child's father is?"

Marissa rolled her eyes at me as she set her phone down. Adjusting her bed, she sat up so she could read me, and I was waiting on it.

"Why do I have to tell you or anybody else anything? I don't owe none of y'all an explanation about what I will have to take care of for eighteen years. You don't need to even come up in here trying to lecture me just because you got a young nigga wit money."

I sucked in some air, trying to refrain from returning her jab. "I was not trying to lecture you. What does Del having money have to do with anything? We are about to be the parents of two babies at one time," I held up two fingers, "you think that's gonna be easy?"

"Oh wow, Mona, y'all are gonna have help. His fly ass mama will be there to help y'all, Jason will be there, and then it's two of y'all. I don't know if Tay is even gonna stay with me now that I slipped up and did this shit."

"Ain't nobody about to make you raise her alone. I love you, Marissa, despite all the crazy shit you have done. I would never let my niece be in this world needing for anything."

She had her head cocked to the side as she stared right past me. My words had little to no effect on her which was pissing me off. No longer able to take it, I put Tavonda in her arms and stormed out of there right past Delano and Tay, who were standing at the end of the hall talking.

"Hold up, man, let me see what's wrong with my wife," I heard Delano say as I stepped onto the elevator.

He tried to run up, but missed it as the doors closed in his face. I wished that I could close everybody out right now just like the doors had done to him.

DELANO

I don't know what Mona was trippin' about, but I certainly was trying my best to be patient. As I waited for the next elevator, I saw Tay walk back into the hospital room with his head down. I felt sorry for him because he had a lot to deal with being that Marissa was a hoe who could not be trusted. Lately, every piece of music he had written had a sad tone to it that I wasn't feeling. I couldn't allow him to waste my time with his crying over some girl who was not worth it. Truth was, I hated her. I played it off well, but I despised the little bitch. I loved Mona and dealt with her only because of that, but I knew that one day I would blow my top around her.

The elevator doors finally opened, and I stepped in. A flood of emotions washed over me when the doors re-opened and I saw Mona sitting in the lobby with her hands covering her face. I walked over and sat next to her before she melted into my arms.

"What's wrong, ma," I whispered in her ear.

People stared and whispered all around us, probably assuming I had done something to her.

"She just doesn't get it, Del. She has that baby in there and... she is not going to be a good mother. We gotta do something."

I almost let go of her at that moment. There was no way I was about to take care of a child that was not mine from a woman I couldn't stand. I couldn't tell her that right now without making her more upset, but she had me fucked up for real.

"Don't worry, Mama, I saw Tay walk back in the room. I think they are gonna work it out."

She looked up at me with red-rimmed eyes so full of hope that I prayed I was right. I wiped away her tears and convinced her to go home and get some rest.

As soon as we got home, I got her up to bed and made her a fruit salad. Finally, when she fell asleep, I slipped out of the house to take a breather. I needed a breath of fresh air and some male conversation that didn't entail babies, emotions, relationships or anything remotely close to that. I hit the remote and climbed into my black Aston Martin V-12 Vantage. As the engine roared to life, I carefully backed out of the driveway.

Fumbling in my pocket for my phone, I finally located it and called pops. I needed to clear my mind and my head about some shit I had going on for a while now. I was getting closer and closer to telling my wife, but I was worried it would cause her to miscarry. Once again, I had been forced into a situation that I wanted no parts of because of my family.

"Hello," Pops answered, sounding cheerful.

"What's up, Pops?"

"Shit, nothing much. I'm just sittin' over here thinking about driving down to Mobile to go fishing. Remember my buddy Gus used to have a place down there that sat right on the gulf?"

I smiled at the memory of him taking me when I was younger. It was one of the happier moments we shared when I caught a fish bigger than his.

"Oh yeah, I remember Mr. Gus. How is he doin' anyway?"

"He is in hospice right now. They had found some cancer in his head but it was too late. I was gonna tell you, but you had so much goin' on at the time." I said a quick prayer in my mind for Mr. Gus as I listened to pops talk. "What you and Mona-Lisa got goin on?"

"She is at the house. I am actually just driving around trying to clear my head."

"Clear your head? What's the problem son?"

I took a deep breath and eased up off of the gas which I realized I had been flooring.

"There is just so much pressure on me right now. I don't know if I am coming or going, and I can't really do nothing but keep it to myself for the time being. My wife wouldn't understand."

There was a long silence as he read between the lines.

"In other words, you need to talk to me, huh?" I nodded my head yeah then it dawned on me that he couldn't even see me. "Bring ya ass on then and head down with me. I'll be back tomorrow."

"I'm on my way, Pops, and don't be tryin to get us no nasty ass Coronas. That's white boy shit," I remarked and hung up the phone.

# CHAPTER 3

TAY

The nurse came in to take the baby as soon as I walked through the door. I reached for her, but she rudely shoved right past me.

"I called them to get her because I was tired. I thought you were gone, sorry."

"No worries, I just had to take me a lil smoke break." I walked over to the bed and moved her hair off of her forehead.

"Tay, I know you don't wanna hear this, but..."

"Shhhh, don't even say that because you are not sorry. You can say you apologize but don't ever say you are sorry. I just wanna know what you expect me to do? Do you even know who the daddy is?"

The blank look on her face gave me the answer that I needed. She didn't really have a clue. I guess this was what I got for trying to turn a hoe into a housewife. My baby mama, Star, never stepped into my affairs, but she did warn me about this.

"Does it even matter who her father is? You have been the one going to this doctor and that doctor with me. You was the one feeding my late night cravings and holding my hair up when I had to throw up. You are her father as far as I'm concerned."

I looked at her sideways after her little speech because I was far from being moved by it. I was not about to sign a birth certificate for a child that I knew wasn't mine.

"What is it, Tay? Why are you looking at me like that?" I leaned down and kissed her forehead to prepare her for the blow she was about to be dealt.

"I understand where you are coming from with everything and I appreciate that you have such a good attitude about it. However, I can't just let this shit slide like this. I held this in because I thought you would make a better decision for yourself, but I know this is Petey's baby." Her mouth dropped open dramatically just like I knew it would. "Don't act so surprised, Rissa. I saw all the damn texts and shit where y'all was meeting up with each other. I didn't think you would be stupid enough to be fucking me and him raw, so I guess I gave you too much credit."

The angry look she gave made me want to knock fire from her. *How she gonna have an attitude?"*

"So are you saying that we are done, Tay? Is that what you came back up here to say? I am sorry about what happened, but I don't regret my baby, not for a minute. If you don't sign the birth certificate, then it just won't be signed. But don't get it fucked up like you are doing me some favor because I can take care of her on my own."

I had to laugh at the remark, especially when I realized that she was serious. "Lil girl, you don't even take care of yourself. You live in your sister's big ass house where you pay no bills. You wouldn't know how to survive out here by yourself. I'm mad as a muthafucka, but I got every right to be. I sacrificed my damn dignity to be with you. I rescued you from a nigga that treated you like yesterday's trash and you repay me by laying up with a nigga that brags about how many times you were loving the crew? Come on now, we both know that you are the type of chick that needs a nigga to make her feel important, and I'm not here for that. I love you and I will take care of Tavonda, but I won't be signing a damn thing."

She hit me with a slow clap. "That was quite the show. You want to make me out to be the villain? You wanna tell me why baby mama is calling and texting you in the wee hours of the morning? She couldn't be talking about nothing but dick at that time of morning and—"

I handed her my phone. "Taviar been sick with a fever so she was calling me to update me on his progress. You really need to realize that every woman ain't a dick fiend like you." She glanced down at my phone and I could tell that she felt stupid. "Go ahead and look through it. Me and my baby mama get along well and I don't feel the need to apologize for that. She understands me and I understand her, so we don't have the issues that most people have. I don't have to hide nothing that we talk about."

"Oh really? Then maybe you can explain why she sent you a pussy pic," she said, throwing my phone at me.

I caught it and looked down at the screen. There was a pussy pic on the phone, but it wasn't Star's. I knew she would never believe my explanation, so I didn't offer one. I turned around and walked out so she would have the space she needed to get her mind right. Meanwhile, I was about to head over to Star's to have a little chat with her.

# CHAPTER 4

MONA-LISA

I woke up feeling slightly refreshed. After using the bathroom, I called Del to make up for how I acted at the hospital. My emotions had been all over the place lately. I could tell that he was becoming frustrated with me, even though he tried his hardest to play it off. Two calls with no answer irritate me slightly. *What the hell is he doing that he can't answer the phone?* I slid my swollen feet into the Chanel slippers Constantina had bought me. I felt like she had overdone the twin's nursery with all of her couture designers, but at least she had stepped up. Since Mama had moved back home, I had barely heard from her. Daddy had been working so hard that I rarely even saw him, but we did make an effort to talk and text each other all of the time.

I stood at the top of the staircase, dreading the long walk. Del laughed at me, but I was dead serious about installing an elevator. I had broken a light sweat by the time I got to the end of the stairs.

I heard *Trap Queen* playing as I turned to walk into the kitchen. Following the sound to the living room, I picked up a cheap android phone from the coffee table. It looked like one of the cheap throwaways my cousin Ray used to always have. My first thought was to set it down, but the curiosity in me caused me to open it. Scrolling through the call log, I didn't recognize any of the numbers. I was about to put it down when something told me to look through it some more.

I looked through the messages but there were none, so next I went to the gallery. I was pleasantly surprised to find several pictures of a beautiful little girl with long brown curls flowing all over her head. The first few pictures were of her as a baby, but the more I scrolled the more she grew up. The last picture showed her blowing out candles on her 8th birthday cake.

Just as I sat the phone down it rang again. I felt nosey answering someone else's phone but figured it may have been important.

"Hello," I answered hesitantly.

"Um, hey... may I speak with Delano please?" The feminine voice asked politely.

"He's not here, but you can speak to his wife," I replied and plopped down on the couch.

## TAY

I took a deep breath before walking into the house.

Starkisha looked up from the magazine she was reading. "The food is on the stove," She said and went back to her magazine.

"I didn't come over here to eat. Why the hell you sending naked pictures to my phone like that?" She laughed as she placed her magazine down. "Your lil' girlfriend must be in her feelings. I actually sent it to you by mistake. I was trying to send it to my brother. I was messing with this Dominican chick and she let me take a few pics, so I was sending them to Tank and I accidentally sent you one."

"I highly doubt it was an accident, but whatever you say. That caused some confusion this morning with—"

"Tell your chick she need not be so insecure. I don't want you, and you established a long time ago that you didn't want me. As far as I'm concerned we just homies that got a kid together."

We both had to laugh at how ridiculous that sounded

"That's why I couldn't deal with you. You think too much like a nigga," I replied, walking toward the kitchen.

It had become like a routine for me, I would argue with Marissa and then somehow I would end up back over here. I had love for her because she took excellent care of my son, but there was nothing about her that appealed to me physically. Not to mention, Star wasn't exactly into men these days anyway. I always knew she had that curiosity about her when were together, but now she was completely out there with it. I was cool with it as long as she didn't confuse my son.

I stared at the fried chicken, cabbage, pinto beans, and cornbread that sat on the stove and began making my plate. Just as I grabbed a chicken breast, I felt two tiny arms gripping my legs.

"I got you, Daddy!" Taviar yelled as he looked up at me.

I set my plate down and scooped him into my arms. "Yeah, you got Daddy. You always gonna have Daddy, you know that?"

He nodded his head yes and I kissed him on the forehead before placing him back down on his feet. As soon as he hit the floor he ran into the living room with his mama as I took a seat and dug in. Marissa could barely season food let alone cook it, but I loved her ass anyway. I just didn't know if I loved her enough to take on another man's responsibility. After all, she didn't do anything for my son.

## MARISSA

I brushed Tavonda's hair as she laid on my chest. Mama had been calling up here getting on my nerves, and Tay's ass hadn't been back since leaving with an attitude. I mean I had fucked around on him, true enough, but at least I named Tavonda after him. Besides, I was the one who went through all the pain to get her here. As far as I was concerned, he was being dramatic as hell about the situation.

My chest was on fire because Tavonda had sucked so hard once she latched on. I needed Mona-Lisa up here, but didn't want to hear her lecturing me with all that self-righteous shit. She acted like her and Delano had it all because they had money. Truth be told, I could still get him if I wanted to.

After getting Tavonda's hair the way I wanted it, I grabbed my phone to snap our picture. *They gon' be all over this one on the book.* I started to be petty and tag Tay's baby mama, but he had no idea I knew who the fat bitch was. The only thing cute about her was the way she dressed because the girl had a bad ass wardrobe.

As I waited for my notifications to go off, I scrolled through my phone. Petey's number beckoned me to call him but I just couldn't take the rejection right now. I wanted to see how things would play out with Tay anyway. As soon as my notifications chimed, I hurriedly rushed back to Facebook. I was disappointed when I saw I only had three likes, but that frown faded when I noticed I had an inbox message.

I thought my heart would stop when I saw who it was from.

Damn, you ain't got no rap for a nigga? After all we been through I can't believe you tryin to act brand new. I see you had a lil' baby, so I guess I should say congrats but I don't mean it because shawty shoulda been mine.

You dealin with that fuck nigga Tay now huh? I feel you though because you needed a nigga you could run and that damn sho wasn't the kid. Anyway I was just sayin wassup. You can still use my number, I ain't fucked up about what went down.

I reread the message two more times to make sure I wasn't trippin. Todd had some nerves writing me after all he caused. I started not to respond, but I knew he would see that I had read his message so I kept it short and sweet before deleting the conversation. The last thing in the world I needed was to start back fucking with him. A knock on my door broke me away from my thoughts.

"Ms. Marissa, it's time to take the little one back to the nursery."

I poked my lip out as Nurse Gallagher reached for my baby. I couldn't wait to get out of here because I was paranoid every time they took my baby to that nursery.

I was relieved to get a little bit of a break, though. Sitting up in my bed, I stretched as I tried to figure out what I wanted to do, being that I was so sore and not supposed to be moving around too much.

I was just about to call Mona when my door swung open slowly. As soon as the figure appeared I reached for the nurse button, but I wasn't nearly fast enough.

TAY

After I left Star's house I decided to suck it up and go back to the hospital. As fucked up as I was about the situation, I also knew that I would be less than a man if I left her now. One thing I knew about Petey was that he was not about to step up. I lost count of how many girls I've seen him and Todd go through. They used to be on some running a train shit after we left the studio, but I wasn't on it. Marissa was the first and only girl I ever messed with that had a fucked up reputation.

I plugged my phone up to the usb port and hit the *Spotify* app on my phone. *Blackberry Molasses* was playing, so I sang along with it as I cruised down the highway. Halfway through a Robin Thicke joint, I realized I hadn't stopped for gas. I pulled into a Shell station and retrieved my debit card before exiting the car.

"Appreciate it bruh," I said to the guy who held the door open for me to walk in behind him.

He hit me with a head nod before heading to the bathroom.

"Damn, nigga, how you gon' come to a public place and shit it down like that?" he joked to the person inside the men's bathroom.

I shook my head as I waited in line to pay for my gas.

"Yes, sir, how can I help you?" the small coffee colored girl asked looking up at me with violet contacts.

"Let me get forty on six, please," I replied and handed her two twenties.

She tried to touch my hand but I pulled back too quickly. I couldn't stand thirsty ass women.

"Tay, is that you, nigga?" the familiar voice asked.

I spun around to see Petey walking up with the guy from the bathroom. He looked monkey as hell in a pair of lime green joggers with a black leather strip down the side. His feet looked like boats in the matching foamposites and the fitted tee looked like some shit a teenage girl would wear.

"What up, tho?" I replied casually. I didn't know what his angle was because he had never made a point to speak to me before.

"Man, I should be congratulating you. I saw the baby on Facebook.

*He tried it.* I thought to myself. "Yeah, I appreciate that, man. I'm on my way back to the hospital now, "I said as I backpedaled to the door.

His smile taunted me as he nodded his head. I tried to hurry up and pump my gas before he walked out of the store, but no such luck. Him and the Donkey Kong looking nigga he was with walked over to burgundy Magnum parked a pump over from me. I gritted my teeth as he hit me with a fake smile while he gassed up his car. I didn't bother to return it.

As soon as I was done pumping, I peeled out of the gas station feeling like a sucker. The nigga had just tried me, and I felt like a punk for letting him get away with it. But I knew how he was cut and he wasn't worth me losing my temper. With my mind now fucked up, I decided to take a smoke break before I went up there and said the wrong thing to Marissa.

I pulled up to the club parking lot and parked in the back by the dumpster where nobody could see me. Opening up the console, I grabbed my Crown Royal bag where I kept my loud. I rummaged around further until I found my grape flavored wraps and proceeded to roll up. I had been trying to kick the habit so I could get a decent job, but every time I tried to do right, evil presented itself.

That nigga, Petey, had gotten on my bad side real hard with all that fronting. I wanted to make him feel me so bad, but then again, he wasn't worth the issues he would bring to me. I happened to know that he played with the police, and my background wasn't exactly squeaky clean. I remember the day I overheard him talking to Mark about setting up Todd. I personally didn't care too much for Todd, so I played Helen Keller like I didn't see or hear shit, but I took note that day that Petey was one that couldn't be trusted.

I licked my lips in anticipation, and just as I was about to light up, a knock on my window made me drop my blunt. I looked up to see Constantina standing over me, so I opened the door.

"Hello, Tay. I saw you parked out here when Phillip was taking out the trash. I hope you were not about to smoke marijuana out here like some common thug." I was caught, so I didn't really know what to say. "Come inside and smoke like a gentleman."

Her long ponytail blew in the wind as she strutted through the parking lot in a black Valentino pantsuit. I didn't know a woman in this world who could rock a pair of stilettos like her. I followed her inside the club where the workers were cleaning and getting ready for the night.

Her henchmen watched me as I followed her into Delano's office. She sat down behind the desk like she owned, it and I couldn't help but notice the neat stacks of paper all over the place.

"I consider myself to be lady like, but I think I need to go back to the seventies for a moment." She reached for my blunt.

I just smiled and handed it to her. To my surprise, she retrieved a lighter from her bra and lit it.

"I never said I was a saint. Don't give me that look," she remarked before taking a long pull on the blunt. "You look like you lost your best friend today. What's going on? And don't give me that bullshit about nothing bothering you because it's written all over your face."

I shifted in my chair as she handed the blunt back to me. "I just got a lot of shit going on right now, excuse my language. This situation with Marissa ain't gonna work for me. I can look past the fact that the baby ain't mine because I knew she was a hoe, but—" She wagged her finger at me cutting me off.

"I don't like to use such language. Men screw around all the time and don't get labeled for it, so let's not use that term. Go on."

I laughed nervously but those blue eyes pierced right through me.

"As you know, me and Marissa are together. She had our baby, or what I thought was our baby. The shit is about to cause a whole lot of problems because I got an idea of who the daddy is, and I don't like the nigga." She sucked her teeth lightly but didn't interrupt me. "I want to do the right thing and take care of this baby because she is innocent in all of this, but part of me will always be mad that she isn't mine."

Constantina rubbed her hands together thoughtfully. "I honestly do not see the problem." I gave her an 'are you serious' look. "I missed out on

Delano's whole life because of fear. I knew my father would never accept him and I was afraid that the rest of my family wouldn't. The most he has ever let me into his life was managing this nightclub that brings back bad memories for me. If you want my advice, I would say that you take care of the bambina like she belonged to you. Don't make her suffer for the sins of her mother. And as far as Marissa goes, that is the relationship that you can choose to easily walk away from."

I exhaled the smoke that was beginning to burn in my chest. She had a damn good point about everything she said. I did love Marissa, and niggas raised kids that didn't belong to them all the time. I would not be the first or last. She winked at me as she reached for the blunt. I smiled as I handed it to her. She was always so damn mean looking and serious that I never realized how cool she was until now.

"You look like you are contemplating what I have said. I hope that is the case."

I slowly rose from my seat. "You gave me a lot to think about. I appreciate it. I don't have parents to help guide me."

She blew out smoke through her nostrils. "I don't have a child to guide, so I guess we are in the same boat. Stay a while, would you? It's not often I get to converse with a young man."

I sat back down as she passed the blunt back to me. My phone began to ring, but the look of disappointment that crossed her face caused me to silence it. I had a bad feeling that I would regret doing that.

# CHAPTER 5

DELANO

"Son, you been awfully quiet since we been on this road. You okay?"

I looked over at Pops, not wanting to lie, but not wanting to tell the truth either. It was time to address the elephant in the room that he knew nothing about.

"I'm just a lil' stressed out, Pops. Some shit been on my mind that will probably fuck my whole life up once it comes out. On top of that, Mona-Lisa has been on my fuckin nerves real bad lately. I'm a compassionate man, but all this crying and mood swings is killing me. I can't leave the house without her having a conniption.

"Man, these women are a trip when they carrying. Your mama was mean as hell when she was pregnant with you. You can't hold it against her, son. You gotta get used to the mood changes and all that other shit that comes with it. You got a whole lot goin' on at one time, which is where I think the problem comes in at. That's why it's good you're getting away for a day."

My guilt set in slightly because I hadn't called or texted Mona-Lisa that I would be gone. I didn't want to hear her mouth.

"Yeah, well my main problem isn't Mona right now. What she got goin' on is minor in comparison to what I am facing."

He shot me a puzzled look as he sucked the foam off the top of his beer. "Lay it on me, son. You got legal problems or something?"

"Nothing legal just yet, unless my wife decides to divorce me."

"Why in the world would she do that? What did you do?"

I had to smirk at the panicked look he gave me.

"It ain't what I did. It's what you and Constantina did," I said, cutting my eyes at him.

"Del, what the fuck are you talking about?"

I grabbed my phone and scrolled to my gallery.

"You wanna tell me who this is?" I questioned, holding the phone in his face. He swerved as soon as he looked at it.

"I uh…" he stammered.

"My last year of my bid was especially hard because me and Mona was beefin', and then one day I get a letter from a fuckin' ghost. You ever got a letter from a ghost pops?"

He kept his eyes on the road, but no words left his mouth.

"Y'all led me to believe that my first love died, then all these years later she come writing me to tell me we got a fuckin' daughter. I had to take my first view of my child in a damn prison. How you think that made me feel? What the fuck else you been lyin' about?"

"Del, you was still in high school. What was I supposed to do? I knew you wasn't ready to be nobody's father."

I clenched my fist because I wanted to steal on him so bad. "I can understand you thinking I wasn't ready, but it wasn't your place to make that decision for me. Then you bring Constantina into it when she didn't even raise me."

"What you want me to say, son? I—"

"I don't want you to say nothing because everything that comes out of your mouth makes me wanna swing on you." He drained the rest of his beer before throwing the can in the back seat. "If you feel like you can whoop my ass, I can pull over. You mad and all, but don't get beside yourself because I will fuck you up out here."

I took off my Movado watch and placed it in the console. "You do some fucked up shit to me and then threaten to whoop my ass, then I say convert me nigga, go ahead and make me a believer."

My face warmed up like it was in an oven as he smirked at me.

"If you want this hand to hand combat then you can get it, but what will it solve? What exactly did Dannity tell you anyway since she wanted to run her mouth?" He asked.

"She told me enough for me to know that you, Connie, and her mama concocted that bullshit ass story about her being killed in an accident. The shit all made sense though because they acted like she wasn't at the hospital, and you said it was because they couldn't tell us nothing since we weren't family. Then I was too distraught to go to the memorial service, but how the fuck y'all pull off the graduation shit?"

He lowered his head slightly. "You haven't learned by now that money talks? Your mother handled that part of it. She had a talk with the principal so you could accept her diploma."

I stared at this nigga as he spoke like cool-hand Luke. He honestly didn't see anything wrong with what they had done.

"I got an eight-year-old daughter whose life I missed out on. After the way you claimed my mama abandoned me, why would you make me do the same thing to my own child?"

"It was a bad ass decision. I realize that now. When I found out that girl was pregnant, I lost it. I thought y'all would've been more careful than that."

I crossed my arms. "What, you mean like you and Constantina? That weird shit y'all had going on fucked me up. You had me believing the bitch just tossed me to you and had nothing else to do with me when all the time you was still dealing with her. All them magazines and posters you had of her boxed up in the garage, but kept showing me the same old faded ass picture. I don't wanna be like neither one of y'all when it comes to mine!" My chest heaved up and down as I tried to control my rage.

"It was a long time ago and the cat is out of the bag now. What do you want me to do, Delano? I can only apologize so much, but as a man, I will not kiss your ass."

I rubbed my hands together slowly as he tried his best to make me see his point of view.

"Kiss my ass? That's what you got from all that? I just wanna go the fuck home right now. My wife don't know where I'm at anyway."

He gave me a hard look but I wasn't worried about none of that. As soon as we came up to the next exit, he got off and looped back around. I hit my Spotify app and clicked on my TI playlist before sliding in my earbuds. I didn't want to hear shit else he had to say.

Not to be outdone, he turned up his radio and drowned me out with Anthony Hamilton. I cracked my knuckles and gave his ass a warning look before I punched the radio as hard as I could. It abruptly stopped playing and I smiled at him with a satisfied grin. *Get mad if you want to and pull this car over, nigga.*

# MONA-LISA

I paced the floor in my living room with my hand on my head. The phone call I just had seemed surreal to me. I could not believe that Del had hidden this from me. I started to call my mother-in-law but I didn't really want to involve her in my business any more than I had to. I loved Constantina, but she had a way of making me feel like I was weak just because I wasn't as strong as her. To make matters worse, I was extremely nauseous and nothing would come up when I tried to vomit. I had called Daddy, but of course, he was at work. Calling Marissa wasn't an option because she was on some childishness right now. It was times like these that really made me miss Leslie. I had learned through a mutual friend that she had lost her baby. It was rumored that Todd had beat her and caused her to miscarry. I still didn't wish that on anybody.

I felt like going through my house and destroying everything of value, just like my heart had been destroyed. *This coward ain't even got the guts to call me back.* Against my better judgment, I took a deep breath and dialed Leslie's number, hoping she hadn't changed it.

"Hello," she answered sleepily. I started to hang up but the damage was already done.

"Hey Leslie."

"Mo, is that you?" The tone of her voice had changed drastically so I knew she was happy to hear from me.

"Yeah, it's me."

"I thought you ain't fuck with me no more. Please don't be calling to rub it in about my baby." I placed my hand on my chest in offense. "I would never do that,

Leslie. I don't hate you, I just hate what you did." There was a silence on the line, followed by sniffling.

"I said I was sorry, Mona. What else you want me to say? I can't kiss your ass forever. I did some fucked up shit and I am deeply sorry." She began to sob so heavily that I felt myself tearing up to.

The line became quiet as I listened to her soft sobs. I didn't want to care as much as I did, but I couldn't help it. Leslie didn't really have anybody and I knew that. Her grandparents didn't understand her, and no female could be around her more than five minutes without wanting to kill her.

"Leslie, I just called to see if you were okay. I wouldn't wish a miscarriage on anybody... not even you. The truth is, I am lightweight miserable right now. I'm in this big ass house and I feel like a prisoner not being able to go anywhere because I'm on bedrest."

"Girl, I am so tired of being in this house with my grandparents I don't know what to do. I was gonna move on campus but granny got sick, so I had to stay here and take care of her."

"I'm really sorry to hear that. Tell her I will be praying for her."

"I will do that. Thanks for calling, though, because I really needed to hear from you."

There was another awkward silence as I searched for something to say.

"Well, I will let you go, Mo, but please don't be a stranger."

I was so in need of some girl talk, and since Marissa was still in the hospital, I figured it couldn't hurt to hang out with Leslie.

"Wait a minute, are you busy right now?"

"Naw, not really. I just gotta go get Granny from dialysis why, what's up?"

Before I could talk myself out of it I asked Leslie to come over to the house since I was supposed to be taking it easy. It would be like old times to have somebody to talk to that understood me like no other. Besides, I was tired of holding the grudge on Leslie. Years had passed, and it was definitely time to bury the hatchet.

Two hours later, I was opening the front door for Leslie. "Well damn, I didn't expect all this. I knew Delano was doing good and all, but y'all living like Jay Z and Beyoncé up in here."

I giggled at Leslie as she twirled around in a circle, taking the house in. She looked flawless in a purple and gold mini dress, gold half jacket, and purple peep-toe thigh high boots. She wore her hair tapered on the left with wand curls on the right that fell right below her breast. The tribal tattoos on her collar bone and nose piercing were all new to me. I was lightweight envious of how good she looked. Her light brown eyes were lined heavily with black liner and her nude lip stick was popping. I was definitely jealous

"Damn, Mo, you really doin' good for yourself." She grabbed me into as tight a hug as she could muster with my belly in the way.

"This is all my husband's doing, Les. I spend my days sitting in here trying to figure out what I want to buy online or watch on TV because I can't go no damn where."

"Why can't you go anywhere?" she asked curiously.

"The doctor is concerned about the twins. He says that they are so much riskier than a regular birth, and I've messed around and got gestational diabetes."

"You gotta be careful with that, Mo."

She walked over to the couch and parked her thick five-foot frame. "Honey, I would take all of this any day of the week than live with my old ass worrisome ass grandparents. Here I am, twenty-four and still living at the crib while you are living life like its golden. Plus, you still sexy as hell, pregnant and all."

Her compliment made me blush, being that the last thing I felt right now was sexy.

We walked to the balcony overlooking the backyard so she could light her blunt. The whole time she was talking, all I could do was think about how fancy-free her lifestyle was. She was able to still go out, travel, and come in when she wanted to. I love my husband, but I would be lying if I said I didn't miss my freedom sometimes.

DELANO

The tension in the car was damn near unbearable for Pops, but I was cool. I was concerned that Mona wasn't answering my phone calls after she had blown me up. I called Constantina to see if she could check on her but got no answer there either. I tried not get paranoid, but I was worried. I had just switched to my *Jagged Edge* playlist when a call from Dannity came through. I didn't feel like talking to her so I let her hit the voicemail.

Shortly afterward, she left a text. **You need to answer your phone**. As much as I used to love her, I could barely stand her now. I leaned back in my seat as much as possible before allowing my mind to drift off.

*"Aye, pretty nigga, what you lookin' all long-faced for?"*

I looked over at my celly Roland who was drawing a tattoo design on an envelope. "Ro, this is the worst possible time in my life to get this news. I am about to get married next week and this shit comes to me left field like this."

I had re-read the letter a million times hoping that the words would change, but they never did. I had a fucking 2-year-old daughter who was calling another nigga daddy.

"Look here, at least she told you. I mean I got six knuckle-heads at home and only 2 of 'em is mine, but I love 'em all equally. Kids are a blessing, no matter how they got here. It's fucked up that you ain't know, but the best thing is you still got time to tell your fiancé so y'all can go in on a clean slate."

I stared down from my bunk at him like he had lost his mind. There was no way Mona would ever forgive me for this, and I couldn't risk losing her.

*"That's not an option, Ro, and you know it. Women are sensitive ass creatures that can't handle the truth they beg for. Plus, this is a hell of a story this girl came up with. How I know she ain't lyin'?"*

*Staring into the mesmerizing blue eyes of Delainey I knew there was no way she could be anybody's but mine. Lying down on my side, I read the letter one more time as I spread her pictures out in front of me.*

*Dear Delano,*

*I don't really know how to start this off, so I guess I should just do so by telling you who I am. You know me as Dannity Sheldon and we were in love once. Before you get upset, let me first explain that I had nothing to do with any of this. We were kids and I got pregnant, so my parents did what they felt was best. They concocted the story about the car accident to hide the fact that I was pregnant and refused to abort my baby. You gotta understand that I was the great black hope in my family and they didn't want anything to tarnish that.*

*When I left you that night, I went home and cried. I told my mother that you proposed and she flipped out on me. The next thing I knew, I was being driven out of town and they came up with that story. I had to go live with my Aunt Sylvia in North Carolina and miss our graduation and everything. Once I found out what they had told you I felt like it was better that I stayed out of your life. When Delainey was born I was in that delivery room by myself feeling so lonely and afraid. Aunt Sylvia has been a Godsend helping with Delainey, but my parents barely even acknowledge her. All they can think about is the fact that I decided to be a mother.*

*I don't want any money from you or anything like that, I just want you to know your daughter. I have a wonderful boyfriend named Lawrence that she calls daddy, but I want her to know the TRUTH. Both of you deserve the truth. I finally had the courage to look you up and when I googled you, I was surprised to find that you were in prison serving time on a murder case. I figured there was no time better to reach out to you than now.*

*Please tell me that you will be in her life. I will enclose my phone number and address at the bottom of the letter if you decide to contact me. I see your face every time I look into hers. Please don't let your emotions keep you from loving her.*

*Love Always,*

*Dannity Sheldon*

I held onto that letter for two days before I decided to write her back. The first time I talked to my baby girl on the phone I knew I could never turn my back on her. If I was honest with myself, I would have to admit that hearing Dannity's voice still did something to me. She was my first love and the only one I ever saw myself with until Mona came along.

"We about 30 minutes away," Pops announced, breaking me out of my thoughts.

I snatched my headphones out and set them on my lap. "Just drop me off to my car please."

"Are we gonna go through another spell of not talking to each other?" he asked.

I let out a long sigh. "I don't really know what we about to do. All I am worried about right now is my little family and how I'm 'bout to have to fuck it up with this news."

He lowered his head a little when he turned back to face the road.

MONA-LISA

As the sun crept into my window, I realized that Del had not come home at all. Sitting up in bed, I stretched before lowering my feet over the side of the bed. I barely had time to make it to the toilet before my bladder relieved itself. After washing my hands, I walked into the bedroom and grabbed my phone. I was stunned that Del had finally called back, but it was much too early to cuss him out.

I remembered that Leslie had spent the night when I smelled eggs and bacon as I eased down my huge staircase.

"Les, what you got goin' on in here?" I asked as I walked into the kitchen.

"Girl, I figured I may as well make something in this big ass kitchen since I know I'll never have one like it. I got butter pecan pancakes, omelets, bacon, turkey sausage, and fresh fruit."

My eyes scanned the food neatly plated on my center island. She had definitely showed out.

"Damn, Les, who is gonna eat all this? I know I'm eatin for three, but I don't even think I can eat all this."

She giggled as she removed the last omelet from the frying pan. "Girl, I am higher than gas prices right about now. I don't know about you, but I'm about to smash."

She turned off the stove and climbed onto a bar stool. I followed suit and started fixing my own plate.

"I really am glad you called me, Mona. You are my only friend, and it was hell having you mad at me. I guess life paid me back by keeping me confined in the same position I was in when you left. You, on the other hand, got everything going for you. A fine ass hubby, beautiful home, nice cars, and now you are about to complete it with twins."

She truly had no idea how wrong she was, but I didn't trust her enough just yet to tell her my business. Part of me wasn't convinced that she was as sincere as she came off.

"Girl, there is a lot of responsibility that comes from having all of that stuff," I replied, biting into my sausage.

"Girl, like I said, I would take all of this in a New York minute over what I got goin' on. Losing my child has haunted me these last few years. I would have a six year old right now, Mo."

She lowered her head to hide her tears as I reached over to squeeze her hand. "Les, I know how I felt losing my first baby. I wish I could tell you the grief goes away but I would be lying."

She wiped her eye before biting into a forkful of omelet. "It serves me right after all of those innocent babies I had sucked out of me at the clinic. My hoe ass should have kept my legs closed, and I wouldn't be in this predicament." Dabbing at her eyes with a napkin she continued to eat.

"Let's talk about something happy," I said, desperate to change the subject.

She pretended to think real hard. "I think I am going to take up journalism in school and do something with my writing. You know I always kept my journals and stuff around the house. I'm actually working on this lil' documentary with this guy who is submitting it to the Sundance Film Festival. I been thinking about getting into adult films, and he has been filming me going on auditions and stuff."

My eyebrows lifted so far up that I could have sworn they had left my face for a few seconds.

"Adult films? Why would you want to do porn, Les?" She bit into her bacon loudly. "Last time I checked, I didn't have no rich niggas checkin' for me. I got this bad ass body, I love the D, and I need some damn money. My grandparents got a stash but they are probably not gonna leave me nothing as much as I've disappointed them. As far as I know, they plan on giving everything to charity."

"Do you really think they would do that when they practically raised you?"

She rolled her eyes and popped her lips loudly. "Mo, not everybody has a family like yours. Anyway, you seem really down. Are you sure nothing is going on? If I was in here living like this, I would have my fine ass at the spa everyday getting my nails and toes done, then I would be cashing out in the mall."

Leslie hadn't changed a bit. All she thought about was material things, and maybe it was because she had no responsibilities for real.

"Girl, all can think about are these twins. It seems like one is on my bladder while the other one is pushing on my spine."

Noticing the way she looked at my stomach when I said that, I changed the subject sensing the change in her mood. I didn't mean to be insensitive. When we got back around to talking about relationships I managed to cleverly dodge everything she asked about Delano. I was saving everything I had to say about him for when he walked his ass through the door.

# CHAPTER 6

MARISSA

"Why you lookin' like you seen a ghost or sumn, and where is this baby that's sposed to belong to me?" His light-skin and slanted eyes looked even better than they did the last time I was riding him in his basement. The gold grill was new, but he was fresh as usual in his leather racing jacket, black skinny jeans, and black and green Moschino fitted tee with the matching sneakers. Instead of his signature fade, he wore an even with 360 waves spinning around like helicopter blades.

"Why are you here, Petey?"

His nostrils flared as he walked over to the side of my bed.

"You post this kid on Facebook and think I wasn't about to connect the dots? Why the fuck you ain't tell me?" he asked, jabbing his index finger into my cheek. "You thought you was gonna pass her off as that nigga Tay's?" I swallowed hard afraid to say anything. "You bout a dumb bitch if you thought you could pull that off. She look just fuckin' like me, plus she got my complexion."

"I was gonna tell you, P, I just didn't have the chance."

SLAP!!!

Instinctively, I reached up to grab my stinging face. I could not believe he had just put his hands on me, but I knew better than to scream as his eyes threatened me about what would happen if I did.

"Where you stayin' at? How you gon' provide for her? I know you don't think I'm about to let another nigga raise my seed." I was still reeling from the slap as he continued to fire off questions at me. "If this baby belongs to me, I'ma take her away from your hoe ass and let my mama raise her because you damn sho ain't fit to be nobody's mammy. Where she at anyway?"

I choked down the sob dying to escape my throat. I was terrified to let him see my baby, thinking he may try to kidnap her.

"So you don't hear me talkin' to you now?" He snatched me up by my hair just as the nurse opened the door. He released me just in time to keep from being seen.

"Hey there, I didn't realize you had company. Are you up to feeding your little one right now?"

I looked up at Petey who was glaring at me with the death stare.

"Yeah, she is ready," he answered for me.

The nurse looked at me for approval and I nodded my head slowly. As soon as the door closed, I flinched, thinking he was about to hit me again.

"Straighten yo dumb ass up before she come back in here thinkin' I'm beatin' your ass. I should be mad at myself for sticking my dick in some public pussy anyway. Pushing my still swollen feet to the side he sat down on the bed facing me. "You let that nigga sign the birth certificate?"

I was too afraid to answer him, which was a dire mistake. He looked around before pressing his hand down into my abdomen. Too afraid to scream, I bit my bottom lip as I tried to pry his hand off of me. It felt as if my staples were scraping my insides. Once he drew blood he finally let up.

Disgusted at the sight of my blood, he rubbed it on my gown before washing his hand in the sink. Just as he was drying his hand, the nurse came back in with Tavonda who was fully alert.

Petey reached out for her, but the nurse carried her to my bedside and put her in my arms.

"I will be at my station if you need anything," she asserted before switching past Petey, looking him up and down before exiting the room.

"That bitch like to got cussed out. Let me see my lil' mama."

I nervously handed my baby over to him, half expecting him to do something evil like drop her. Instead, his face lit up like Christmas as he carefully cradled her in his arms. He sat in the recliner by the wall cooing and playing with her. I watched him as he counted her fingers and toes. *He is going to fight me tooth and nail for my baby.*

## TAY

I left the meeting with Constantina feeling better about myself. I took another blunt to the head and woke up feeling refreshed. I called Marissa as soon as the sunlight peeked through the blinds but got no answer. I decided to grab her some garlic chicken from Little Bangkok. After getting my hygiene on point, I got dressed and walked out of the bathroom, tiptoeing to keep from waking up my son. Even though me and Marissa had moved in with Del and Mona, I still felt odd sleeping there without her.

"Where you going so early, nigga?" Star asked wiping her eyes.

I held my finger up to my mouth, signaling her to keep her voice down. It was no use though because Taviar sat up next to her. I gave her a nasty look as I walked into the room and picked him up. "You did that shit on purpose, didn't you?"

She laughed at me and shrugged. "I know you ain't goin' nowhere but up there to see thotzilla and that yella baby. I thought I taught you better than to chase these hoes. You need to let me pick you out a chick. What you want, a long-haired, thick red bone?"

I handed my son back to her. "You real funny, Star. Last time I checked, all your chicks came out the strip club."

"Those just be my moneymakers. Who gon' turn down a chick that get paid every night? You know I like nice shit."

I glanced around her bedroom, and true enough, she had a doper sneaker game than any nigga I knew. All of her shoe boxes were stacked along the all in rows four boxes high since her closet couldn't hold all of them.

"I happen to love her and—"

She made a crucifix with her hands. "Don't utter that word around me. You know me and love don't get down like that."

I chuckled at her before leaning down to kiss her forehead. "You are crazy as hell. I'll see y'all later."

I kissed Taviar on his head before exiting the room and letting myself out the back door.

After grabbing Marissa's food, I headed over to the hospital. I didn't know if she would even talk to me, but it was worth a try. The last thing I wanted was a repeat of my last visit.

****

After I finally found a parking spot, I grabbed Marissa's food and headed inside. The nurses greeted me politely as I made my way to her room door. I held my breath as I slowly opened it. I was not prepared to see Petey holding my baby girl in his arms as Marissa looked at him lovingly. *This nigga is in here playing lullabies on his phone.* They didn't even notice me standing there, they were so caught up in what they had going on.

I felt like a shot went through my chest as I slowly closed the door back. They never even looked up.

"Does anybody in here eat garlic chicken?" I asked the nurses at the station.

"Honey, broke as I am, I would eat you for lunch," a white-haired nurse remarked.

I handed her the food and walked to the elevator. My pride was wounded and I felt like even more of a sucka for signing the birth certificate. As the elevator descended to the first floor, I struggled to get myself together. The only thing for me to do now as face the reality that we were done.

# CHAPTER 7

DELANO

Me and Pops had a few words when he dropped me off to my car last night but I didn't give it to him half as bad as I was about to give it to my mother when she waltzed up in here. I sat up and stretched before raising up to lower the bed back inside the couch. I had slept in my office because I knew it was too late to bring my ass home. Mona was going to be beyond mad when she found out about everything, so I guess I was biding my time a little bit. It still messed me up that Dannity had allowed herself to go along with all this madness. No matter how innocent she made herself out to be, I still felt like she could've done something differently.

The only thing that kept me from choking her ass out was the fact that my daughter was always present. All I know is that I want to be with Mona, but if she doesn't accept Delainey then we were going to have an issue. On the flipside, I had to be willing to understand if she didn't.

I grabbed my phone, remembering that Dannity had called me yesterday. I had planned to pick up Delainey soon like we had planned last week, but she had a way of changing her mind at the last minute if I didn't want to include her. I snapped the rubber band on my hair as I dialed her number. I really hoped she wasn't about to get on my nerves right now.

"Hey Delano," she answered after the first ring.

"You called me?" I asked impatiently.

"I didn't mean to disturb you, but I just thought you should know that Delainey is running a fever so it may not be a good idea for you to come see her right now."

I sighed in frustration thinking about the shitload of toys and clothes I had hidden in my office closet. I wanted to see her little face light up when I brought them to her.

"Damn, I wanted to see her, but I want her to feel better, though. You need me to bring her some medicine or something?"

"Nah, I think she is good for right now. Lawrence brought her some children's Tylenol a few minutes ago."

I tried to hide my disappointment, but the fact that another man had to take care of my child was a hard pill to swallow. I had already missed enough time in her life without having to think about her calling another man daddy and looking at him to take care of her.

"Well, if she needs anything else, please don't hesitate to call me."

There was a long pause, which made me think she had hung up.

"Delano, I know that your wife has probably called you by now, but I swear I thought she knew. I would have never said anything if—"

"What do you mean you never would have said anything?" She got quiet but I wasn't having none of that. "So, that's why my wife ain't picking up the phone. What the hell did you say to her, Dan?"

"I just kinda told her about Delainey and—"

"You gotta be shittin' me! You seriously did that? I bet you couldn't wait to run your mouth, could you? You would do anything to get back with me, but that has been done. When you decided to go along with their lie you lost me forever and you need to understand that. You had not right to tell my wife anything—"

"If you think I'm about let you handle me then you are mistaken," She interrupted. "Do you love her? If you love her like you put on, then you would have told her."

Her question caught me off guard because it was the last thing I expected her to ask me. "I love her enough not to hurt her. What we had was years ago and we have both moved on, so what difference would it make who I love?" For some reason I came off as defensive, even though I wasn't trying to be.

"That's not really an answer, but whatever. I never ever forgot about you all of these years. The way I left has always consumed me with guilt, but Del, I had no other choice for real. My hands were tied."

"Dan, I don't want to hear that, you—"

I was startled by my office door slowly opening. Constantina walked in and flipped on the light. She grabbed her chest when she saw me.

"Delano, I didn't know you were here. Why are you undressed like you..." Her voice trailed off as she eyed my clothes on the floor. "You slept here?"

I set the phone down, not even bothering to hang up. "Yeah, I slept here, it ain't like I can go home. I take it you ain't talked to Pops."

She closed the door behind her before placing her attaché case on my desk.

"I haven't talked to him, but that still doesn't answer why you are in your underclothes."

I slid on my pants. "I am in my draws because I didn't want to face my wife. Looks like I got some news she may take a little bad." She looked confused just like

I knew she would. Those bright blue eyes bore into mine, searching for answers.

"You look lost. Let me take you back to my senior year in high school when I got my girl pregnant. Does that ring a bell?" A barely audible gasp escaped her lips. She ran her hand nervously over her perfectly coiffed ponytail.

"So you know?"

"Yeah, I know. I found out while I was in the pen. I kept the shit to myself for Mona's sake, but baby mama took it upon herself to tell her, so now I'm fucked up."

Constantina walked toward me but I backed away. "Delano, your father panicked and when he called me, I—"

"You tried to save the day with your money, right? All of a sudden you wanted to play mama? My life was fine before you walked into it and tried to buy your way in. As far as I'm concerned, you could've stayed your ass across the ocean with the rest of them muthafuckas that wanted nothing to do with me!" I saw a glimmer of what I knew was a tear, but she was too stubborn to let it fall.

The door flew open and two of her henchmen walked in. "You okay boss?" The tall, slim, one asked with his hand on his hip.

"Kino, everything is okay."

"Hold up. You walkin' up in my shit like you on my payroll. You and this other fake ass good fella better get out of my office before I make you use what you got on your hip."

He walked closer to me but his buddy stood right there. We were nose to nose when Constantina wedged herself between us.

"Like I said, be the fuck up out of my office before I get mad. Take homeboy wit you and take her too."

"Please, let me teach him a lesson real quick," Kino pleaded.

In the blink of an eye, I pushed Constantina out of the way and snatched his gun off of him. I didn't even aim it at him, but I set it on my desk instead.

"Teach me a lesson now," I challenged.

"Kino, please let me have a moment with my son."

He seemed almost relieved as he backed up and stood next to his friend, who still hadn't uttered a word. He looked like he wanted his .38 back but I knew he wouldn't like the way I gave it back to him. I waited for them to leave before I turned my attention back to her.

"I never meant for any of this to happen. I think you should let me speak to Bella because..."

"Don't do me no favors. Matter of fact, I don't want you doing anything for me anymore. I don't need you helping out here or at my house. What was I thinking, trying to include you in my life? You are worse than Pops."

She waved a perfectly manicured finger in my face, "I am nothing like your father. I could never be as low-down as he is. If you do not want me to be around, then I will respect that, but you will not keep me from my grandchildren. I accept that I have hurt you, but I do not allow anyone to speak to me the way that you have, so let this be your first and last time."

She spun on her heels and walked out of the door while I stood there looking stupid. It was then that I realized that Dannity was still on the phone. I hung up on her before getting dressed. I was headed to the crib to get this whole ordeal over with.

## MONA-LISA

After Leslie left, I showered and found something clean to put on. Constantina had just called to let me know that she was on her way over and I couldn't let her see me looking a mess. She read me so well that I could never hide when something was wrong. I wanted to ask her if she had talked to Delano. To make matters worse, my bedroom was a mess and the housekeeper was off today. So, I had to waddle my pudgy self around the massive bedroom and clean it, huffing and puffing all the way.

Leslie had kept asking me if I was okay, but I didn't feel comfortable discussing my situation with her since we hadn't talked in so long. I just kept using the excuse of pregnancy symptoms. Now that she was gone, the house was so quiet and still that all I could do was concentrate on what Dannity had told me.

"You are Delano's wife. Wow, this is so awkward. I wanted to speak to you after I first broke the news to Delano about having a daughter, but I didn't have any way to get in touch with you. I don't really know what else to say other than I'm sorry."

I wanted to clown her or find something rude to say, but my lips were not as fast as my mind was. Here I was talking to my husband's baby mama.

"This is all too crazy. I can't believe this.

"Please do not blame him because he didn't know. I was never supposed to tell him, but that is a long story." There was a long pause as I struggled to find the words to say. "Can you please just tell him to call me back?"

"You lay something like this at my doorstep and then have the gall to ask me to have him call you? You couldn't be serious.

*"I'm very sorry. I uh…. I'm sorry." She stammered before hanging up.*

The sound of the doorbell brought me back to the present. I looked at the monitor by the bedroom door, and sure enough, it was Constantina. I was surprised to see her wearing a Pink sweat suit and pink running shoes. I should have known that she had to work hard to maintain that body. Pressing the button to unlock the door, I glanced at myself one more time in the mirror before heading into the hallway.

"Bella aren't you a sight for sore eyes?" she remarked as I slowly descended the stairs. She looked so cute with her hair pulled up into a ponytail. "You could use some sun, why are you cooped up in this house?"

"My doctor told me I had to be on bedrest, so I am stuck in this gigantic prison."

She hugged me tightly. "Bella, this is hardly a prison. You have to just find things around the house that you can do for the time being. One thing you could do is help Delano with some of the paperwork from the club so that he can get a break."

I rolled my eyes in the air as she pulled away from me. I was hoping she didn't catch me, but I wasn't fast enough.

"Tell me what is going on. Is he acting foolishly? Because I will set him straight." My eyes betrayed me and began to fill up. Grabbing me by my hand, she led me to the couch. "What is going on?"

I shook my head but she grabbed my chin, forcing me to look into piercing blue eyes that nobody could lie to.

"I would rather not say right now..."

"You are pregnant with my grandchildren bambino and bambina, so I cannot have you stressing out. What is it that my son has done to you?"

I eased back onto the couch, staring up at the ceiling. This was not about to be easy to say. I took a deep breath before swallowing the lump that had formed in my throat.

"He has a baby."

A look of utter shock fell over her face as she grabbed my hand.

"What do you mean, 'he has a baby'? Who told you that?"

"His daughter's mother called and told me. He had a secret phone and everything.

"I just had this same conversation with my son at the club," she admitted.

It was my turn to be shocked. "You mean to tell me that you knew about this too? You haven't been in his life five minutes and he told you about this?"

"Bella, you don't understand the situation."

I crossed my arms, shooting fire from my eyes as I grilled her. "What don't I understand? The way you and your son conveniently forgot to tell me that he has a fucking daughter! You have smiled in my face and told me how much you loved me like I was your own, but then you lie to me?"

She stood to her feet, holding her hands up in surrender.

"Bella, I understand you are upset, but you may want to watch your mouth before you say something you don't mean."

I laughed right in that bitch's face because she really had me fucked up at this point. "You are standing in my house telling me to calm down? Is that what you're doing?" I paused for emphasis. "The only thing I have to do is exactly what I want to do in the place where I lay my head at. I let you convince me that you loved me so much, when you are no different than my own mother. How the fuck do you expect me to feel right now? Wait, I forgot you didn't even raise your own kid, so you don't know what I am feeling right now."

Her face dropped and I realized I had gone too far, but I was beyond the realm of sanity right now.

"Y'all all got me fucked up if you think I'm going to take this sitting down. I will go back home with my daddy and raise my children on my own before I stay with a nigga that can lie to me our whole relationship!"

She stood there clasping her hands together as I continued to rant. I yelled until my voice went hoarse.

"Are you finished?" she asked quietly.

I shook my head yes, afraid of what would happen next.

"Good. I let you get your point across, now you will listen to mine. You will not interrupt, interject, or intercede, but you will listen. Do I make myself clear?"

"Crystal." I retorted and walked back to the couch.

"You can be a little smart ass all you want because in this situation you have the right to be. However, do not make it a habit or it may cause you problems that you will have no idea how to escape. The first thing you need to know is that nobody was ever supposed to know about this child. I paid that little cunt and her mother a nice amount of money to keep her a secret. My son was still a teenager with his whole life ahead of him and there was no way that me or Dorian were going to stand by and watch him struggle through his life trying to be a father that he was not mature enough to be. I had hopes and dreams for my son, regardless of how his upbringing made it look."

She began to pace the floor as I took in each and every word. I wondered in what world she thought it was cool for a person to disown their child.

"Bella, let me explain something to you that your mother should have a long time ago." I gave her my undivided attention as she sat on the couch next to me. "A woman that is in love will do anything to obtain the object of her desire. She will lie, steal, kill, and destroy until she gets what it is that she feels belongs to her. This girl waited until my son was in prison, at the lowest point of his life, to contact him with the news that she was alive and had a child. Why would she wait until such a time you ask? I'll tell you. She thought that he was so desperate and lonely that he would rush back into her arms and be with her forever."

As much as I hated to admit it, what she said did make sense to me.

"This woman wanted to come back into his life and decided that she would do so by any means necessary. I would love to tell you that this woman is lying and that the child is not my son's, but I would be lying to you. We had DNA done a long time ago and she is definitely his. The decision you make now is on you. No one will blame you if you leave, but if you stay, just know that you will have to join in on this song and dance that she has started because she will not give up if she has come this far."

"You know what I don't get?" I replied, standing up.

I don't get how you just throw money at every problem. Did you honestly think this was a good idea?"

She shrugged. "It's how we do things. Money is a universal language that anybody can speak. So what are you going to do? Are you going to sit here and just give up on your marriage or will you accept what has already been done?"

I cocked my head to the side and stared straight through her. I finally realized what type of family I had married into and I wasn't feeling it at all.

"What you have shown me by coming here is that you will always use your money to get you out of sticky situations, and to me, that is not being a woman. Hell, that's not even being grown. You asked a teenage girl to hide the fact that she was pregnant so that your son wouldn't have any responsibility. You wanted him to walk away from her with a clean break just like you did with him. As far as I'm concerned, you are no better than my own low-down ass mother."

I could see her jaw clenching, but I no longer cared about being respectful. "I wish I had never met you or your son and entered into this fucked up family full of secrets and lies. This shit is like a bad movie plot with y'all. I mean, I couldn't even make some shit up like what y'all have going on. There is no way to fix anything that's been done, but one thing I can fix is this."

I pulled off my wedding band and engagement ring and hurled them in her face before storming up the stairs. By the time I reached the top, I heard my front door slam. *Good riddance then, bitch.*

DELANO

I was nervous as hell as I stood in the florist shop. I let the owner put together an arrangement all the while knowing that no amount of calla lilies, roses, or gardenias, would make this any easier. I thought about calling Mona first, but it occurred to me that she probably wouldn't answer. *Why the fuck did my parents have to fuck over me like this?*

According to Pops, it was Dannity's mother calling him and panicking that made them decide it was best to send her away. He then called Constantina, who wired him the money and even paid for her prenatal care. Not one of them considered how hard I was going to grieve over my girlfriend, and they didn't even allow her to have a say-so. I'm more upset that she still didn't try to reach out to me on her own after everything happened, though.

I paid for the arrangement as my phone started ringing. I damn near threw it when I saw it was Dannity calling again. I ignored her ass and headed to the car. She was really starting to become a thorn in my side. To drown out my thoughts I turned up the radio listening to Keyshia Cole crying about yet another nigga that did her wrong. I pulled up to the house and all of the lights were out. My heart dropped as I clicked the remote on the garage. When it opened and I saw Mona's car, I was relieved.

Pulling in beside her, I lowered the garage door and entered the house through the mud room. It was in complete darkness, which immediately worried me because Mona was never one to be in the dark by herself.

"Mona!" I shouted as I felt for the light switch. She didn't say anything so I continued to walk around the house, peeping into each room. When I flicked on the light she was lying in the bed looking at her phone. "So you didn't hear me calling you?" I questioned.

"I'm sorry, I must not have understood what you were saying because I'm not fluent in bullshit!"

"Mama, if you would let me explain..."

"Explain what? What you wanna explain to me?"

The wild look in her eyes with her hair standing on top of her head was new to me. I knew she would not be rational, so I just opted to walk away when I was stopped short by her snatching my hair. I landed on the bed where she wasted no time straddling me. Her punches were so hard and swift that I barely had a chance to grab her wrists.

"Are you fuckin' serious right now? You need to calm your lil' ass down and think about what you're doin!"

"Fuck you! I don't have to think about shit! Let go of me!"

While I had her wrists, I slid from under her and pinned her down to the bed. I could feel my face burning from where she had scratched me.

"I understand you are mad, but you—"

My sentence was cut short by the most disrespectful shit ever. I felt the spit roll from my forehead down the bridge of my nose. I had to close my eyes and do a mental countdown before I did something to her. I released one of her wrists so I could wipe the slime off of my face.

"You need to call your father right now," I said calmly, releasing her other wrist.

She sat up in the bed rubbing her wrists as she glared up at me. "Call my father for what?"

"Because if you don't leave my gotdamn house right now voluntarily, you may leave later involuntarily." I turned to walk into the adjoining bathroom when I felt a hard object hit the back of my head. When I turned around I saw a crystal jewelry box on the carpet by my feet.

"This is my house too, so you can miss me with that! I'm not about to go nowhere so you can move in that bitch and her baby! I'm staying right here, and ain't shit you can do about it!"

"You right, this is your house too. I'll let you have that, but what you won't do is back me into a fuckin' corner. I can't be here with you right now because you already tried me. I tell you what, you stay your ass here and I'll leave."

"You ain't goin' nowhere!" She lunged at me, but I pushed her on the bed effortlessly.

"Mona, I don't want to hurt you, so please quit trying me. You gonna fuck around and make my babies come tonight if you don't stop."

She placed her hands on her hips as she struggled to catch her breath. "You weren't too worried about your babies when you was out wining and dining your ex and her child."

"You can kill all that right now because she is my child too! What are you talking about, anyway? Who been wining and dining anybody?"

"I been texting lil' miss Dannity, and she made it clear that you and her and the lil bastard child been hanging real tough like a family. Is that why you been having your mama work at the club? So you could spend time with your girlfriend?"

"I never heard a more ignorant statement come from you. The situation ain't ideal, but it is what it is! Whatever she is feeding you is just to piss you off, but you're too stupid to see it. I'm not begging you to like the situation because I don't, but you damn sho better learn how to live with it because that lil bastard you speak of is my seed, and I'm not turning my back on her. If you want to stay Mrs. Dawson, then you need to learn real quick how to accept the hand we been dealt."

"And what if I don't? You gonna leave me for your ex?"

My nostrils flared as I looked down at her. I felt like a bully standing over her like I was, but I had to get my point across. We stood there in strained silence for a few minutes before I walked into the bathroom. I sat on the edge of the garden tub trying to get my thoughts together when the door few open. I wasn't quick enough to dodge the vase of flowers I had just bought her before it connected with my head and sent me flying backwards. The impact of hitting the porcelain tub head first gave me an instant headache.

*She ain't worth the jail time,* I convinced myself as I struggled to get up.

# CHAPTER 8

MARISSA - Two Days Later

Even though Tay hadn't been back to the hospital, I was ecstatic to be finally going home. Petey had been up to the hospital every day to see the baby, but the made sure to let me know that he planned to get full custody of her. I knew with his record that it would be a long shot, but I also knew that he had a support system that would help him. He would never be crazy enough to go to Delano and Mona's house, so I would finally be free of his crazy ass.

"Okay, I think we got the last of everything," Ms. Constantina replied as she raised up from buckling Tavonda's car seat into her truck.

Her driver helped me into the back of the truck before helping her in, and we were on our way. She pulled down the visor to look at me.

"Marissa, you truly have a beautiful little bambina. I hope that you are ready to take on all of the responsibilities of raising her."

"It's gonna be hard, but I think I can manage. I appreciate you coming to pick me up because Tay is still mad at me."

Her eyebrows shot up in surprise, making me wonder if I had said too much. "I am guessing it is because he is milk chocolate and this child is French vanilla." I shot her a knowing smile. "He will soon get over it as all men do. When he thinks about what he is missing out on, he will step up and accept that she is his in his heart."

Her words comforted me because in my experience I had found just the opposite. I thought about Ivory with his sweet ass. He was horrible to his wife and sister and was only mildly interested in getting to know me. I hoped they bent him over every day in that prison, but then again I didn't because I knew he would enjoy it.

We rode the rest of the way in silence as Constantina texted vigorously on her home. Upon pulling up to the house, I noticed there were several cars parked outside. She whispered something in Italian to her driver and they shared a good laugh as he pulled up behind a purple PT Cruiser. She helped me out of the truck as I looked around for Tay's car. I was disappointed when I didn't see it.

The driver grabbed my baby and my things for the hospital as I painfully struggled up the few steps to get to the front porch. We could hear music and laughter as I rang the doorbell.

Jason answered the door with a glass of wine in his hand.

"Baby girl. how you feelin'?" he asked, grabbing me up into a warm embrace.

"I feel a little sore, but I am okay."

"Come on in." He stepped aside, greeting Constantina warmly with a kiss on each cheek before taking the car seat from her.

I thought it was odd that she didn't walk into the house, but that thought quickly left when I realized how beat up I looked in comparison to everyone else.

"Where is my beautiful niece?" Mona ran in and hugged me.

"Jason just took her."

Mona gave me a look before walking off to find him.

"My baby just had a baby and still lookin' as good as ever."

I turned around to see Mama walking down the staircase in a fitted gold one strap dress. I wasn't mad at her gold peep-toe pumps though. *She is definitely trying to get Jason back.*

"Hey Ma, I don't know about looking good, but I sure feel good with this baby being outside of me."

She kissed me on my cheek, brushing her long lashes against my face.

"I am sorry I couldn't be there, but me and my boo bought you a little gift."

I allowed her to lead me into the dining room where everyone waved and spoke. After a quick greeting, she pulled me into my room. I noticed that my bed was still made like Tay had not been there, but not wanting to spoil the mood, I just plopped down on the bed.

Mama sat next to me and crossed her legs. "I know that a lot has transpired since I left, and I just wanted you to know that I am sorry for the way I treated you and... my whole family. I had to move back home to get over Jason divorcing me. He had every right to—"

"Ma, I thought this was about a gift," I interjected. I did not want to hear about her and Jason right now. She reached down between her breasts, trying to grab something. "Umm, whatever you got in there is probably extremely sweaty, so um, no thanks."

She laughed as I sat there with my nose wrinkled. "You mean you don't want this?" she remarked, handing me a wad of cash. "I was gonna give this to you in front of Mona, but you know how jealous she is of you. She got this nice house and all, but that girl is so unhappy. If I had a husband that was thank-you-Jesus fine and he put me up in a home like this, I would be on my knees every day for him."

"That's a little too much info, Mama," I replied, taking the money from her. "So who is this boo you mentioned earlier?"

Her green eyes lit up like emeralds. "Honey, he is a cardiologist, chile. I met him at work and it was love at first sight. He is a little bit older than me, but I don't mind a seasoned vet as long as his bank account ain't retired."

"Cardiologist? So you got you a man with some real bread then, huh?"

She winked at me. "Girl, you better know it. He had this dress custom made for me and the shoes were imported from Italy just for the occasion. You know I couldn't half- step with Jason being here. There are a lot of successful people in his family, and if you play your cards right, I may be able to hook something up."

"Ma, you know I have a boyfriend, and—"

"But where is boyfriend? Why didn't he pick you up from the hospital? Why is he not celebrating the arrival of his little princess?" I didn't want to tell her the truth, so I thought of a quick lie.

"He is actually working tonight, so I asked Ms. Connie if she would come and get me."

At the mention of her name, Mama turned her nose up. "I bet that heffa couldn't wait to get over here and parade around in front of Jason. Little does she realize, the nigga will never get over me, so she will always be second best." I thought it was cute that Mama was still jealous, but I knew that the last thing Jason wanted right now was a relationship, especially with her. "Well, put that money away and come on out here to meet your future stepfather. I shook my head as I pulled out the top drawer next to my bed. All of Tay's underclothes were missing.

# TAY

I looked down at my phone for the millionth time. I don't know why Marissa kept calling me. In my mind, I wondered if she saw me at the hospital and just didn't care. I always had the feeling that maybe she wasn't attracted to me as much as she was to the other niggas she had dealt with. I parked my car and slid my phone in my pocket before stepping out. The parking lot at Motivations was beyond crowded, but thankfully all the employees had designated spots. Delano looked out for his people like that. Despite the cool weather, I saw mini-dresses of every color and style as I made my way to the side entrance.

"What's up, Scarface?" Rico joked as I approached him.

Normally, I would laugh at his tall, goofy ass, but tonight I wasn't feelin' it. I walked straight past him and inside the club. The mixture of perfume and cologne was damn near nauseating as I slid through sweaty bodies grinding against the wall. I slid up into the employee bathroom and unlocked my locker. After throwing my bulletproof security vest over my black tee, I locked it back and stepped in front of the mirror.

Tonight was the night of our $10,000 shakedown contest, which had been Constantina's idea, believe it or not. She figured it would be a way to bring in more heavy hitters with deep pockets, but Del wasn't really feeling it. He knew it would be trouble when Mona found out, but they seemed to be on the outs lately, anyway. I ran my hands over my dark waves as I admired myself. The thing with me is that I knew I was ugly, which was why I made sure I stayed in the gym and dressed nice.

"Damn, ugly ass nigga, you gon' stay in here all night or you gon' do some work?" my co-worker, Rondell, asked as he burst through the door.

"Man, tell your baby mama to hold on, I'm looking for my singles." We both laughed.

"You got me, bruh, but on the real. I hope Tamara's ass ain't out there because I'm behind in child support."

I shook my head before pushing him toward the door. I gave Del a head nod as I passed him to go to my post at the front door. He had a drink in his hand which was very strange because he never drank anything harder than vitamin water. Once I reached the front door I frowned when I saw that the line was wrapped around the building and we were almost at capacity inside.

"Damn, it's about time somebody got out here to let me in. I signed up for this shit two weeks ago."

I looked up at Rondell, who had a Suge Knight mug across his face. His thick, tan arms were crossed and he leaned back in his 'cuss a bitch out' stance. I knew it was about to be trouble if I didn't intervene.

"My apologies, love, we had shift change. What's your name?"

"Raven and not like Symone either. I am Raven like the bird in Edgar Allen Poe's poem."

"This bitch," I heard Rondell mumble under his breath to some girls standing behind the velvet ropes.

She twisted her neck around, giving all of them a look that miraculously made them mute.

"Like I said, I am Raven like the bird in the poem, but these bum broads around here probably never heard of it. Anyway, can you rush up wit' ya lil' list because I got money to make."

I scanned her tootsie roll colored body that was covered in a tight canary yellow baby tee, stonewashed skinny jeans and matching yellow Bali tennis sneakers. Her long dreads were colored turquoise on the tips and were pulled up into a high ponytail that cascaded down the sides of her face. My hand shook as I scrolled through my phone for the guest list.

"Some time this year would be good, hun. I mean it is cool out here."

"So bitch why you ain't put on a jacket?" Rondell thundered, stepping in front of me.

I hated how disrespectful he was, but there was nobody better to have behind you in a fight.

"Not sure who you are talking to, but you need to come correct before you get ya bologna colored ass sliced up out here!" she replied, dropping her duffle bag.

He stepped toward her and she didn't budge, so I took the opportunity to insert myself between them.

"Rondell, let her in, man. I saw her name on the list," I lied.

He sucked his teeth hard before pulling the rope back to let her walk past. I knew I would hear it for the rest of the night. It took us two hours and three fights to get the crowd under control.

"Aye bruh, I'ma grab a bottled water from the bar. You want one?" I offered.

Rondell looked up from his phone long to nod yes before going back to what he was doing.

I stepped inside the club just in time to see a purple light bathe the stage. I walked over to the bar slowly, trying to see what was going on.

"This the chick I came to see. I been following her from Ohio, cuz."

I looked at the goofy looking yellow dude who made that comment and shook my head. *Some niggas are too thirsty. I should offer his ass one of these waters.*

"A'ight y'all, we getting into the middle of this thang. Y'all still makin' it rain, or is ya pockets dried up?" the DJ remarked over the mic.

Half the club threw up money in response. I tipped Phillip the bartender and was making my way back to the front door when I heard *Jupiter Love* playing. The whole club went black for a second, which instinctively made me turn around.

When the lights came back on, there was a girl center stage sitting in a chair with her back to the audience. As soon as Trey Songz began to sing, she leaned back in the chair, causing it to fall to the stage with such grace that it barely made a sound.

She slid off the chair and kicked it to side before flipping over onto her stomach and lifting her ass in the air to bounce to the beat. I knew I had been gone from my post too long, but I couldn't step away from the show. She stood to her full height, displaying the men's button down that she wore. It clung to her perfect hour glass frame as she loosened her tie, throwing it across the stage. I sucked in my breath as she slowly unbuttoned the shirt to reveal purple rhinestone pasties with a matching G string that was only visible from the front.

She kneeled down on all fours, crawling to the very front of the stage before spinning around to flex each cheek, one at a time. Men and women both cashed out on her as she slid off of the stage and into the lap of a man sitting in the very front.

"You get paid to watch the show?" Delano asked from behind me.

"My bad Del, I was—"

"Don't trip, just get back to work," he replied before disappearing into the crowd.

He was never that short with anybody so I knew he had something on his mind. The rest of the night was a blur of fights and drunk strippers. I was more than ready to go home once we had the parking lot cleared out.

"This was the worst idea Constantina ever had. I will never do this shit again," Delano complained after locking the safe. "I never wanted to fuck with this type of crowd, that's why I tried to keep my spot classy. I don't know why I listened to her. I got at least three hundred dollars' worth of broken glass and two stopped up toilets. Not to mention—" He was interrupted by a knock at the door. "Come in," he answered.

I was pleasantly surprised to see Raven walk in with her street clothes on. "I didn't mean to interrupt, but I was trying to see if somebody could walk me out. I don't really feel comfortable walking out of a strange club with all this bread on me."

"I was about to leave, so you can walk out with me," I offered.

"Congratulations on the win, Miss Raven. I would tell you that you are welcome to perform again, but you got niggas turning my club up over you. You are beautiful no doubt, but that beauty ain't gonna fix the damage done to my club tonight."

She lowered her head slightly. "If I didn't need this money, that little plea would make me give it back."

"Ma, you won your money fair and square. And as far as the damage, you better believe I got that covered. Tay, go head and walk the lady out. I'll holla at you later on."

I dapped him up and held the door open for Raven. I tried not to eyeball her ass as she walked, but it was impossible. There was a classiness about her that contradicted everything she had just done on that stage. I followed her to a burgundy Crown Vic that I knew upon sight belonged to a man. The 26 inch chrome rims, limo tint, and candy paint were just not the car I would expect a woman to be driving.

As if reading my mind, she spun around. "This is my big brother's car. He got killed over this piece of shit. I just kept it because it reminded me of him. Anyway, thank you for walking me to my car. Let me find out you a gentleman." She unlocked the door and tossed in her bags before climbing into the driver's seat.

"No problem. You take it easy, lil mama." I backed away from the car, giving her room to close the door, but she stood there as if she was waiting for something.

"So that's it? You not gonna ask me for my number or nothing?"

"Why would I ask for something that I don't really need. I have a girl at home and she is enough to deal with. I don't need another one to make trouble for me. But you are beautiful though, if that's what you wanted to hear." *You are sexy but I don't fall all over any woman.*

She ran a purple stiletto nail down the side of her face as she continued to stare at me. I was starting to feel uncomfortable.

"So you gonna sit there and act like you wasn't staring at me? I saw you walking in and out all night stealing glances at me. You must be feeling some type of way about what I do for a living."

She had hit the nail on the head, but I wasn't about to let her know that. "I need to get home to my son. You have a nice night and be safe."

I could feel her eyes on me as I walked to my car. Once I was inside, she peeled out of the parking lot. I knew right then that it wouldn't be the last time I saw her.


DELANO


"Aye that sounds real good, Del," Tay remarked as we finished listening to his finished song.

"Yeah, it's dope. You did a good job." I tried to be excited about the upcoming show we were doing in Detroit, but my head was still wrapped around my situation.

"Aye, man, I didn't wanna ask, but you been lookin' a lil' out of it for the last few days. You and Mona a'ight?"

Turning off my computer, I looked over to where he sat on the couch. "I could ask you the same thing, 'cause I see you done up and moved out, plus you wasn't at Marissa's welcome home party."

He lowered his head slightly. I guess we were all going through it. At least he wasn't married to his problem.

"Man, I can't with her. She had that nigga Petey at the hospital like they was a happy lil family. I mean what I look like just accepting that? She got me fucked up, Del." I rubbed my beard thoughtfully.

"Well, I never expect much from her, but I got some shit goin' on that might spell the end of my family."

He looked up at me in surprise. "What you mean, boss?"

"I mean that I got a fuckin' daughter that I found out about a few years ago when I was in the pen, and Mona can't accept it. My parents made a fucked up decision and now I gotta live with the consequences of it. It's a long ass story, though."

"How she gon' trip about a kid you had before her if you ain't even know?"

I shrugged. "That's what I'm tryin' to understand. I mean, I know she is upset, but she is making it seem like she wants me to disown my daughter, and I can't do that. It's to the point that we got into it and she claim she is moving out. I don't know what else to do. Everybody been in my ear about Mona being immature, but I thought she would've grown up by now. We seven years in, and nothing has changed about her."

"Damn, man, you and Mona-Lisa been like the fuckin Huxtables to me. If y'all can't make it then what hope do the rest of us have?"

I had to laugh at that as it had never dawned on me that other people envied our relationship.

"We got problems just like everybody else. No amount of money can change that. I just thought that after marriage this would get easier. Mona has always been a little childish, and I used to think it was cute. But now it's time for her to grow the fuck up. Okay, we got an issue. Let's just fix it and move on. If you ask me, her parents sheltered the fuck outta her."

My phone buzzed in my pocket. When I pulled it out, Dannity's face popped up. "Let me take this call real quick."

Tay exited the room quickly as I answered the phone.

"Hey Delano."

"What's up, Dan? How is my little princess doing?"

"She is good. I was actually calling you because we wanted to see you."

"I got a lot of work right now, but maybe this weekend will be better." I relaxed in my chair, propping my feet on my desk.

"Oh well, she was going out of town this weekend with Lawrence's mama."

I wasn't really feeling her being with people who weren't family, but I was still struggling with feeling like I had any say over her.

"Damn. How long is she gonna be gone?"

"She will be gone just for the weekend so we can move into our new place. Lawrence got a promotion so we are upgrading to a house."

As much as I tried to convince myself that I wasn't thinking about her like that, it still made me a little jealous to hear about her boyfriend. The fact that he was around my daughter more than I was didn't sit too well either.

"So y'all on your George and Weezy shit, huh? Congratulations." I tried to hide any traces of sarcasm in my voice, but I doubt I pulled it off.

"Uh, thanks. I wanted to see if I could bring her to see you before she leaves."

"I can meet you somewhere because I don't want her at the club. My house is a whole nother story."

"Okay, well just let me know something. My hairdresser is telling me to get off the phone right now."

After disconnecting the call, I got up from my desk and walked into the bar where Tay sat with the stripper chick from last night.

"I don't mean to interrupt you, but we gonna have to put our conversation on hold until tomorrow. I am about to go see my daughter before she heads out of town."

"Oh ok, well let me introduce you to my... friend, Raven."

I side-eyed him as she extended her tiny hand.

"Nice to meet you again, ma."

"Likewise. This place looks a lot different in the day time. It's nicer than where I usually dance at."

I winked at her. "That's because this is not a strip club. I was just doing something different, but after the mess that was made, I will probably never mess with that again. Nice seeing you again, but I got some business to handle. Tay, let me holla at you real quick before I leave."

He followed me out to the parking lot, and as soon as the door closed, I laid it to him.

"Your business is your business, and you know I stay out of it, but please keep that shit you got goin' on outside of the club. If Marissa brings her ratchet ass up in here tearing my club up, we gon' have a problem."

"Man, it ain't nothing like that. She is just a friend of mine, and she popped up over here, but I feel you."

"A'ight, well, I'll see you later on tonight."

We dapped each other up as I climbed into my car. I texted Dannity to meet me at Bambinelli's. For some reason I got slightly nervous as I drove over. I shook off the feeling as I pulled into the parking lot. I was relieved when I walked inside and she wasn't here yet. I grabbed a corner table in the very back and looked over the menu while I waited.

I had just taken a sip of my water when she walked in. Looking her up and down, I realized my nervous feeling had been dead on. *This is about to be some shit.*

MONA-LISA

"Okay, I think we got the last of it, Daddy."

He looked at me with his brows furrowed as he took the box out of my hand and placed it into the U-Haul. I had been listening to his lecture for hours, but I had my mind made up. If Delano thought he was about to treat me like shit because of a mistake he made in his past, then he was in for a rude awakening. I hopped into the passenger side as Marissa watched from the front door. I told her that it was her choice to stay, but I was leaving. Me and Delano were sleeping in separate rooms and not even speaking, so I was over being in this house with him.

When I called Daddy he had tried to talk some sense into me, but what could he really say when he had a failed marriage? Luckily, Mama and her boyfriend were holed up in some hotel because I didn't want to have to face her right now.

"Put on your seatbelt. Look, Mona, I don't like being dragged in the middle of this. You and Delano married each other, and that means that y'all work out your problems without dragging everybody else into it. Didn't you learn anything from me and your mother? I don't know what the hell happened between y'all, but you movin' out is a bold ass move. How are y'all gonna raise these babies together? Have you even thought about that?"

Daddy pulled out of the driveway as I thought about what to say.

"We have both agreed that this was for the best," I lied.

"So you mean to tell me that he is okay with you just up and moving out while he is gone to work? I don't believe that for one minute. I never thought I would see the day when your sister was more mature than you."

That stung a little bit especially when she had her own thing going on, but I didn't want to run her business to him.

"Can we please just drop it? As soon as I have my babies, I will find me a job and get my own place. I don't need Delano or his money."

He turned and looked at me like I was stupid. "So you think you can do this all by yourself? Mona, raising kids is not something that—"

"Can we just please talk about something else? I have made my mind up. I am leaving him and there's nothing that you or anybody else can say to talk me out of it."

He snapped his head back toward the road. I knew that I hadn't told him enough to make him understand, but as crazy as it was, I didn't want anybody judging Delano. I was mad at him, but I still loved him and didn't want to throw him under the bus. I turned on the radio and sang along with Jasmine Sullivan. *I'm not scared of lions and tiger and bears, but I'm scared of loving you...*

DELANO

Dannity walked in looking like something out of a music video. Her hair was cut into a sleek asymmetric bob, her generous caramel frame was covered in a strapless orange dress so tight she appeared to have been dipped in it. Red pouty lips accentuated the beauty mark above her lip, while gold stilettos that strapped up to her thighs completed her look.

"Where is Delainey?" I asked, trying to avert my eyes. I pulled out her chair while I waited for her response.

"She is with her daddy right now because I need to talk to you."

I sat down across from her, feeling my jaws clench. "Her daddy is right here, so you mean she is with play daddy."

"She is with the man that raised her, so call it what you want to, but like I said. I need to talk to you."

Her beauty faded to me just that quick. "You not brining my daughter means there is really no conversation to have."

She was about to reply when we were interrupted by the waitress.

"Welcome to Bambellini's. My name is Alecia and I will be your server. May I start you off with something to drink?"

"I think I will just have a glass of water with lemon please," Dannity answered.

"Yes ma'am, I will be right back with that. And, sir, would you like a refill?"

I didn't even know if I wanted something to eat at this point, so I shook my head no. I waited for her to walk off before I went in on Dannity.

"So what is this all about? You walk in here looking like you about to audition for *The Voice* or some shit. Then you don't even bring my daughter." I tried to keep my voice even, but she wasn't making it easy with the smirk on her face.

"Delano, I brought you here tonight to talk about us."

Taking a deep breath, I sat back in my chair. *Damn, Mona is always right.* "What about us, Dan? We ended a long ass time ago when I asked you to marry me and you told me no. Now, all of a sudden you come back in my life surprising me with a child I never even knew about. You realize that I could lose my wife behind this?"

"Here you go, ma'am. Are you all ready to order?"

It was my turn to shoot the waitress a dirty look for her bad timing.

"Give us a few minutes," I replied nastily.

She looked like she was about to cry as she scurried to the other side of the restaurant. I turned my attention back to Dannity who was squeezing a lemon wedge into her water.

"Delano, can we just be real for like five minutes?"

"I can always respect real," I answered, twisting the fabric napkin in my hands.

"The truth is that I never stopped loving you. We were too young to get married when you asked me. I have spent the last few years of my life regretting that decision. It was very hard for me to tell you that you had a child because I didn't know how you would take it. I realize you have moved on and have your own family, and I do too, but just be honest with me and tell me you don't still want me."

I had to think before I answered that because my mind said no but my dick told another story. *Damn I should have changed out of these slacks.*

I took both of her hands into mine. *Damn, her hands are soft as hell.* "Dannity, when you reached out to me I was in a dark place. Mona stood by me while I was locked up, but a whole lot of shit was on my mind. I was fucked up about you hiding this from me for so long and to be honest, any love I had for you kinda disappeared because of it." She tried to pull her hands away but I kept a tight grip on them. I needed her to feel what I was saying so I would never have to repeat it. "Anybody that can hold on to a secret for as long as you and my parents did can't be trusted. Yeah, I am attracted to you, and probably would fuck you real good one last time if I thought I could get away with it, but you could never be my woman again. The spoiled, bratty one that I married has my heart now, and you need to respect that."

She licked her lips seductively causing my dick to twitch a little. I hadn't had sex in a week, and for me, that was a record. I could tell she was about to challenge that by the way she grazed my thigh.

"Del, you don't miss none of this? I never saw your wife but she probably can't do shit with me."

This time I was glad when the waitress walked back over because I felt myself falling for temptation. After we ordered our food, Dannity excused herself to the bathroom. I watched her ass jiggle as she switched past me. *She really need to quit playing with me.*

"Here is your carbonara sir, and for the lady we have chicken cannelloni."

I nodded my thanks and dug in before Dannity got back. I knew I needed to get out of there as soon as possible.

"Damn, you couldn't even wait for me to feed you?"

"I think I still know how to feed myself. You really need to calm down with the flirting because it's getting out of hand." The feeling of a foot running across my lap caused me to slide back in my chair.

"Why you keep playing with me, Del? You want this and I want to give it to you. Stop actin' like we're strangers." I slid my chair further back causing her foot to hit the floor with a thud.

"Ouch. Why did you do that?"

"Can you please just eat your food so we can leave?" I asked through clenched teeth.

Instead of listening to me, she walked around the table and plopped her thick ass in my lap. I looked around the restaurant and all eyes were on us. I felt like Mona would walk in at any moment with the whole crew from *Cheaters*. I tried to push her off of me without drawing too much attention, but the flash of a camera caught us both off guard. *The last thing I need is for this shit to end up on social media.*

"Dan, you got the whole restaurant staring at us. You need to get up."

"If you want me to get up then tell your dick to go down," she whispered, wrapping my arms around me.

"This is some craziness that you're trying to pull, Dan." I shoved her off of my lap and onto the floor.

Just like I thought, she wasn't wearing any panties so her neatly trimmed peach was on display for the whole restaurant. I grabbed my wallet and threw money on the table before storming out of the restaurant. I couldn't get to my car quick enough before I was getting a phone call. Glancing at my phone, I opted out of answering. *Mona, now is not the time for your bullshit.*

# CHAPTER 10

CONSTANTINA

"Dorian, we should have stayed out of this."

I poured myself another glass of wine. Sitting across the table from me, he looked as if he hadn't slept in a week. Grey hair sat matted upon his usually low cut hair.

"Connie, what choice did we have? He was a fuckin teenager. He will stay mad for a little while then he will get over it. I'm just mad at that bitch for not keeping a muzzle on it, considering we had a deal."

I rolled my eyes up to the ceiling. Once again, I had allowed him to talk me into something that had come back to haunt me.

"Maybe so, but you could have helped him raise her, Dorian. You did an excellent job with Delano and—"

He slammed his fist down on the table, causing my glass to jump. "I was not about to have no teenage son raising a fuckin baby! We did the best we could with the situation. You act like we asked the girl to get an abortion or something. All the fuck we asked her to do was stay away. We provided for her and the child, so she didn't want for anything. I just don't understand why she came back into his life. The bitch got a motive and it's probably money."

I drained my glass. "Funny how everyone thinks that I am the one who tries to buy my way out of trouble. It's you that always think in terms of money.

Did it ever occur to you that she may just want her child to know her father? Why does everything have to be about dollar signs to you?"

He looked me up and down before crossing his arms. "The air up there on that high horse you on must be real thin. You forget that it was money that made you choose your career over your own son. I was raising him by my damn self—"

"Oh really? As I recall, Phyllis and Preston had a lot to do with his upbringing until you..." I stopped myself short. I didn't want to rehash the night of the fire. "All I want to do is find some way out of this. Mona-Lisa spoke to me like I was a bitch on the street the other day and it killed me because I had no rebuttal. She was right about everything that she said. We have to fix this before they give up on each other. Could you really sleep at night knowing that we ruined our son's marriage? He wouldn't be happy with anybody else and you know it."

He ran a hand through his closely cut hair while rubbing his face with the other one. "What do you propose we do, Connie? What, you gon' have her killed or something? I ain't takin' part in no murder plot."

I placed my hand on my chest outraged. "You think that's how I solve everything? She is my granddaughter's mother. If I have any hope of ever being in that child's life, then I cannot do it by snatching away the only parent she has ever known. My son hates my guts right now so all I want to do is right the wrong that we committed. You can sit up in this huge house if you want to and pretend that you won't die alone, but I have to take action."

"Connie, don't you think you've done enough? Hell, we can't nothing right now anyway. You gotta let

Delano be a man. I raised him to be independent. He will figure this out."

I certainly hoped that what he said was true because I couldn't stand the way that I felt inside.

TAY

"So you gonna tell me your story?" Raven played with the straw in her coke but wouldn't look into my eyes. I had noticed that she had been averting her gaze ever since we had been together. "You pop up to my job and look around until you find me, and now you sit here and act all shy?"

She placed her straw back into her glass and twirled on the bar stool to face me. What you want me to say? I did come up here and look for you, and that was lightweight creep status, but I only did it because I liked you. You are the first man I have met in forever that wasn't trying to take me home on the first night."

"I told you I had a girl and—"

She placed her index finger on my lips to silence me. You are not happy with your girl. The way that you looked at me showed me that. I know the difference between a lustful gaze and a man that needs attention. You need attention in the worst way." I was impressed with the way that she read me. "I know all about pretending because I have been running all over the country trying to escape what everybody else thought was happiness."

I held up my glass for the bartender, Philip, to refill the gin and juice I was sipping on.

"You know you ain't supposed to be drinking outside of business hours," he remarked, snatching my cup.

I slid him a twenty and turned my attention back to her.

"What are you running from exactly?' I asked. She lowered her head but I lifted it right back up to look into her eyes.

"I was messing around with a nigga that could only show his love by going upside my head." *How could any man raise his hand to something so beautiful?* I wondered. "When I met my ex, I was already dancing. My plan was just to do it for a few years because I really wanted to pursue my dream of becoming an actress or a traveling poet. I had it all planned to move with my sister in NYC, but..." her voice trailed off.

"But what?" I asked softly.

"Grant started trippin about me leaving Ohio. He started coming to the club causing trouble while I was dancing, and he even made me get my hair dreaded up because he thought it would make me less attractive. I let him control me for three years, but when my homegirls told me about the shakedown contest I felt like I had to see if I could win."

I grabbed her hands and held them in mine. "So I just met you, and you leaving me?"

She gave me a cute sideways smile. "Some people are in your life just long enough to teach you something. Plus, you made me feel some type of way when you didn't come onto me, and I know I'm cute," she joked. "Nah, but the thing is I called my sister and I can't get her on the phone. I didn't want to chance driving up there before I spoke to her, so I guess I'm here for a second."

My smile betrayed my need to look nonchalant.

"I guess I could show you around a little bit while you're here," I offered.

"I would like that. Believe it or not, this is my first time here."

"Well, hopefully it won't be your last. Where are you staying?"

She took a sip of her drink before answering me. "I need to save every dime that I have so I parked my car at Wal-Mart and slept in there. I stopped this morning at a gym and took me a shower and stuff."

I shook my head in disapproval. "I can't have you doing that."

"You got your own place?" she questioned.

Technically I didn't because I was staying with Star, but I still had the keys to me and Marissa's old apartment. We had left the more raggedy pieces of furniture behind, but it was still livable.

"I might have a solution for you, but it's not the best of places."

She waved me off. "If you knew some of the places I've been you would know that I'm not trippin."

We shared a little small talk before I got a call from Star asking me to watch Taviar because she had a date. I got Raven's number and made plans to meet up with her later. For some reason I felt the need to protect her like she belonged to me, even though part of me told me to slow my ass down.

# CHAPTER 11

MARISSA

"Girl, you need to hurry up," I whispered to Tavonda who was sucking on my breast.

My chest was on fire. Nobody had bothered to tell me that breastfeeding was going to be painful every time. I rubbed her soft curls as she continued to feed. I was a little upset when Mona left last night, but with Delano busy all the time I could pretend like this big ass house was mine. She had even left her Aston Martin in the garage; in due time I would have the keys to that too.

I tried to feel bad for her about everything that was going on, but the truth was she had brought this on herself. I told her to get rid of Delano the moment he got locked up. It seemed like he had changed by the time he came out of there, just like I knew he would. She put the nigga on a pedestal because he was fine as hell, but so was Todd, and look what type of muthafucka he turned out to be. I had been dodging Petey's phone calls in fear that he would find out where I was staying.

Jason had offered me to come back to the house when Mona left last night, but there was no way I was about to go anywhere near that neighborhood where Petey could find me. I was heartbroken over Tay handling me the way he was, but my daughter was the only thing in this world that mattered. I had already decided I wasn't going back to work at the raggedy ass motel. I was thinking about going to school to get my

CAN certification so I could have something to offer my child.

A knock on my door disturbed my thoughts.

"Who is it?"

"It's Del." I smiled to myself, knowing what he was knocking on my door for. "Come in, Del."

The door opened slowly.

"Wow, you could have told me you had ya titties out, ma," he remarked, covering his eyes.

"Boy bye, this is natural. You sucked on one at some point in your life. Anyway, what's up?" I inquired, making no move to cover up my chest.

He turned toward the wall to avoid looking at me, which I thought was cute. His long waves shined like they had just been washed as they hung loosely down his back. His wife-beater gave me visual access to the angel wings tatted on his shoulders and the thick muscles that lay under them. *He picked the wrong damn sister.*

"So I go up to the bedroom and Mona's stuff is gone. You wouldn't happen to know anything about that, would you?"

"She went home with her daddy last night. You know how much of a cry baby she is."

He spun around, forgetting about my breasts being exposed. "She did what?"

"How you ain't gon' know where your wife is? She called Jason to come get her last night and he came and got her. They had a U-Haul and everything. I thought you knew."

The pained expression that took over his face was a surprise to me. I figured he would be tired of her shit by now, but I guess I was wrong. His eyes watered. *I know this grown ass man is not about to cry.*

Okay, so why didn't you go with her?" He cut those icy as blue/grey eyes at me like this was all my fault.

"I-I didn't want to go back over Jason's house. Come on, Delano, this house is huge. I promise I will stay out of your way."

"Nah, I ain't feelin that. How would it look with you staying here and my wife bein' gone? I can't believe she did some shit like this just out the blue."

"You know better than anybody else how dramatic my sister is. I told her that she was being stubborn, but you know she don't listen to me." I was about to throw her ass all the way up under the bus for acting like a spoiled brat.

He rubbed the side of his face as if still in shock.

"I'll deal with her, but in the meantime you need to keep your body covered up around me and stay out of my way as much as possible." He spun around and walked away before I could find something smart to say.

I was just glad he didn't throw me out because I knew he never wanted me here to begin with. I lifted Tavonda onto my shoulder to burp her. After she was burped, I laid her down next to me so we could take a nap. It seemed that since I had her I didn't have any energy. Just when I got comfortable, the sound of yelling coming from the hallway caught my attention.

I slowly crept out of the bed to keep from waking up the baby. Walking up to my bedroom door I debated opening it, scared that it would squeak.

"So this is what you do when you don't get your way? Why are you so childish? You act like the situation is ideal for me. I am handling it!"

It didn't take a rocket scientist to figure out he was talking to Mona. *Damn, this nigga really don't know how to let go,* I thought to myself.

I climbed back in the bed staring at my baby as he continued to rant on the phone. As I laid there looking at my perfect little girl, I regretted the drama that she was going to grow up in because of my bad decisions. I never wanted her childhood to be as troubled as mine was, and I had cursed her to that. I knew I couldn't hide from Petey forever, and now that Tay didn't want me, I was going to have to be content with being by myself.

All my life Mona had lucked out with everything. She got the better grades, the better treatment from our father, and now she had a damn near perfect husband who looked like he should be on the cover of some European magazine. Once I got with Todd's chocolate ass I thought I was really doing something. I thought I was showing her what it felt like to be second best, when actually, the nigga never really got over her. I had tried Delano once and he wasn't even close to going for it. Rejection was a fucked up feeling.

Tay had the attitude that I wanted and treated me like a queen, but he just didn't have the money to go along with it. What kind of future would I have with somebody that was broke? My thoughts consumed me until I felt myself drifting off to sleep. There had to be a better way of living, and I was determined to find it because for the first time, I had someone other than myself to think about.

MONA-LISA

I paced the floor as I waited for Delano to pull up to the house. I was so mad at Marissa for telling him where I was. He wasn't worried about me when he was at home sleeping in another bedroom. I wouldn't put it past her sneaky ass to be trying to get something started. Constantina had been blowing up my phone, so I'm guessing she knew what was going on too. I was so tired of everybody being in my business. How could anybody not know where I was coming from? Dannity was all too happy to explain to me how she had been writing Delano while he was locked up and had even visited him.

When I got pregnant, he acted like it was the best thing in the world. I watched as he bragged to everybody who would listen about how he was becoming a father for the first time. How could anybody keep a secret like this for years and expect somebody to be okay with it?

"Baby girl, I am about to go to work. You gonna be okay?"

"Yeah, I'm okay," I lied.

Daddy kissed me on my cheek as he walked out of the house with his lunch box.

"Oh shit, Delano, you almost gave me a heart attack. I didn't even hear you pull up," he greeted.

"My bad, Pops, I was just about to knock. Yeah, my baby is pretty quiet when she pulls up, ain't she?" He grinned, looking back at his car.

"Hell yeah. I wanna be just like you when I grow up," Daddy joked.

I rolled my eyes as they made a little more small talk. Delano walked into the house with his hair parted down the middle, hanging down both shoulders. His wife beater clung to his chest, making his muscles pop out more than usual. His basketball shirts did little to hide what he was working with. He never dressed like this, so I figured he had to be going to the gym.

"Ain't you a sight for sore eyes, Ms. Mona-Lisa?"

He closed the door behind him and took a seat on the couch.

"You came over here to talk, so let's try not to be childish or sarcastic right now," I asserted, scooting my feet up under me.

"Okay, so being grown must have a different definition for you than it does for me because I thought being grown meant you didn't run away from your problems. I thought being grown meant accepting that shit don't always go as you planned it." He sat on the edge of the couch twisting his wedding band.

"You have no idea how I feel right now. Until a few days ago I thought I knew who you were. You told the whole world how excited you was to become a daddy when I got pregnant, but the whole time you knew you already were one. In my eyes, that makes you a liar, Del."

He nodded his head slowly. "I can't argue with you on that because you are right. I didn't tell you because I knew you would never be able to handle it. I didn't even know how to handle it. Have you ever stopped to think about how I felt? When I was locked up I thought I would die in that muthafucka because I stayed fighting a nigga to maintain my manhood. When I found out there was a part of me living and breathing on the streets, it gave me even more motivation to get up out of there."

"So having a wife who loved you wasn't enough motivation?"

"Damn, Mona, that ain't the point. You know that I love you and it was my love for you that got me fucked up in the first place. You chose to be here, but my daughter didn't. I have to take care of her. She will have two parents in her life because I never want her to feel the way I felt by having one. Constantina told me that she talked to you and explained what happened, so you know this is not something that I did on my own. What they did was wrong and I will never be able to make up for the time I missed because of her and Pops, but I will be a part of all of my children's lives, and that is with you... or without you." He paused for emphasis.

I had hoped that he had come here to apologize, but it looked like I was getting was an ultimatum instead. "So, you want me to play stepmother, right? You want me to be cool with your baby mama, although it's very clear to me that she still wants you? I don't know what saint you think I am, but I am human as hell, and I cannot just do that. You are asking me to make a decision about something that I cannot do overnight. I love you true enough, but these babies," I rubbed my protruding belly, "are the only children that I feel obligated to."

He clasped his hands together and took a deep breath. "So I guess you got your mind made up. You don't even want to try to work it out, huh?" I looked down at my nails, afraid to answer him because I knew once I said it that I wouldn't be able to take it back. "Well, you gotta do what you gotta do for you. Promise me that regardless of all this, I will still get to see my babies. I mean no bullshit about going to court or none of that because you know I'ma take care of my kids."

"Del, you know I would never try to keep you away from your kids. I am not that type of person."

I could feel my heart breaking as he walked toward the door. If I knew anything about him, I knew how much he hated going backwards. If I let him walk out it would be for the last time. His hair blew back in the wind as he opened the front door. Those blue eyes pierced right through me as he waited for me to say something to stop him.

I stared blankly ahead, not saying anything as he lowered his head and left. I didn't even get off of the couch until his car pulled out of the driveway. I had no idea what I had just done, but I knew I would find out soon. I flipped through a few stations, but the only thing to watch were sappy romances that I had no desire to see. I grabbed my phone and dialed up Leslie for some much needed girl talk.

"Hey, Mo. What you got goin'?" she answered.

"Can you talk? Better yet, can you come over?"

"Girl, I don't have nowhere near enough gas to get all the way out there," she replied, smacking loudly in my ear.

"I'm down the street at my daddy's house. Plus, what are you eating?"

She laughed into the phone. "My bad, I was munching on some sunflower seeds. I was in here trying to study for this exam, but I could use a break. Give me a few minutes."

After hanging up with her, I walked into the bathroom to fix myself up. I didn't need her to see me looking like a mess. My face was a pale mess and my nose looked like a horizontal hot dog as it continued to spread across my face. I found a rubber band in the closet and pulled my hair into a low ponytail so I could wash my face. I had just used the bathroom when I heard the doorbell ring. I quickly washed my hands and rushed to the front door, not bothering to look through the peephole.

When I opened the door, I immediately regretted that decision.

# CHAPTER 12

MARISSA

Tay had hit me up today wanting to see the baby, so I was concentrating on looking good. I wand curled my hair in front of Mona's vanity. Delano was gone as usual, and my baby was dressed and sleeping. After I finished the last curl, I admired myself in the mirror.

Although I was a little thicker than I wanted to be, I still looked good. My dark chocolate skin seemed to have gotten softer since I had given birth, and my naturally long hair fell even further down my back. Pregnancy had done me good, and I had plans on joining the gym as soon as my six weeks were up. I was about to make Tay realize what he had been missing out on. The boat neck, red wrap dress clung much too tightly to my waist and was way too short due to me and Mona's height difference, but I was about to pull it off. It was not really my style, but when I saw Versace on the label I couldn't get it on fast enough.

I heard a car pull up and raced to the window in a panic. Delano would kick my ass if he knew I was wearing his wife's clothes. Luckily, it was only the housekeeper, Valencia.

I didn't need her running her mouth to him but I figured I could keep her distracted with the mess I had made in the kitchen. Not having to clean up after myself had spoiled me, and I was always a bit of a slob anyway. Mona was the damn neat freak.

Picking up the nude Valentino stilettos, I slid out of Mona's room and tiptoed down the stairs. I had barely enough time to get in my room before Valencia was coming into the house. Once she got in the kitchen, I could hear her mumbling under her breath about how filthy it was. I started to go out and check her ass, but my phone started ringing.

"Hey, you here?"

"Yeah. You want me to come in?" Tay asked.

"Uhhh, actually, why don't you just come around to the garage and I'll come out through the side since it's so windy outside."

"You need me to help—"

"I got it. I already got her dressed and everything, but thanks."

I hung up before he could offer any more help. Shoving the too little shoes on my feet, I stumbled around the bedroom shoving stuff into her diaper bag. After carefully placing Tavonda into her car seat, I snuck out of my bedroom, damn near busting my ass.

The cold air hit me as soon as I stepped out of the mud room. I wished I had thought to get her pea coat, but it was too late now.

When the garage door raised up, I was pleasantly surprised to find a Burgundy Crown Vic with a beautiful flaked out paint job and chrome wheels that shined like a diamond. *He must have come up on some money all of a sudden.*

Walking as sexily as I could, I made my way up to the passenger side of the car.

"Hold on a sec, I'll grab her."

Tay hopped out of the driver's seat looking good with a fresh haircut and a black and red Trukfit jogging suit with matching 11's.

"Oh ok, but hurry up. It's cold out here."

He slid around the car and grabbed the baby from me as I opened the passenger side door. To my surprise, a girl looked up at me and waved.

"I will have her back in a few hours. Marissa, this is my friend, Raven."

She spoke to me, but I just stared at her and him. I had put in all this time and effort to get his ass back, and he had brought another bitch to my house. I could have sworn I saw her smirk as I slammed the car door in her face.

"Like I said, I will have her back in a few hours. I just wanted to give you a break. You look good, though," he remarked, getting back in the car.

Before I could scream on him, he was pulling off. I turned around and marched back into the house. I had never been played like that in my life. I didn't even care that he had my baby around this strange bitch; I was more pissed that he had embarrassed me in front of her.

I walked into the house right past the prying eyes of Valencia, who was cutting vegetables. I didn't give a damn if she told on me or not. Throwing myself down on the bed, I wanted to cry, but realized my face was too beat to mess up my makeup. He had officially messed with the wrong one.

TAY

"She was prettier than I expected," Raven commented.

"Yeah, but behind all of that, she has a whole lot of issues. I never saw any girl be so jealous of what somebody else got goin' on."

Raven grabbed my hand and put it in her lap. "I think it's real sweet that you still want to still be involved with the baby, even though you know she isn't yours."

"I know how fucked up my life was without having either one of my people around for real, so I want to make sure she never has to go through that. Plus, I know her daddy, and the nigga is a piece of shit. Besides, my lil boo is named after me." I looked back at my baby girl who was sleeping peacefully next to her brother, who was also knocked out.

"You have a real odd life. On one hand you got a baby by a chick that like girls more than you do, and on the other hand you got this chick that kinda sorta ain't your baby mother. I see I ain't the only one with a complicated life."

I ran my hand over my waves as I pulled up to the traffic light. "I could say I made mistakes because I didn't have my parents around, but that's giving them to much credit for my fuck ups. Me and Star came from the same kind of background and we were just homies that ended up sleeping together a few times. We knew that we didn't wanna abort the baby even though we were young, so we just did what we had to do. As far as Marissa goes, I thought I could build something with her. Get her to quit using her body as an invitation for heartbreak, but she was stuck on being with somebody more attractive."

Raven gave me a sorrowful look. "I don't think you are unattractive. You got a few lil scars, but so what? That builds character, in my opinion."

I tried not to smile too hard, but I had never had it put to me like that. I was far beyond what most women would consider attractive. My lack of height, acne-scarred skin, and up until recently, my braces were always a turn-off.

"Why are you staring at me like I said something wrong? Your personality makes you beautiful, and the tragedy is that she doesn't see that. My ex, Grant, is that tall, muscular, light-skinned nigga with light eyes and pretty hair that most women would kill to be with, but his personality is so ugly."

I took in her words as I pulled into the Wal-Mart parking lot.

"Why are we stopping here?" she asked.

"We need to get a few things to make sure you are comfortable," I replied, opening my door.

She helped me get the kids out, and I couldn't help but notice how we looked like a family as we walked in.

# CHAPTER 13

DELANO

"Are you going to stay mad at me forever, son?"

I ignored Constantina, who was sitting on the corner of my desk. I continued to go through the liquor invoices. A perfectly manicured hand snatched the paper from me.

"It is very rude to ignore your mother when she is speaking to you."

"Constantina, don't flatter yourself. My mother was killed in a fire years ago, or did you not get the memo?"

She placed her hands on her hips as she looked down at me. "As I stated, I understand that you are mad. Me and your father had no right to interfere in your affairs, but we were looking out for your best interest. Have you taken that into consideration at all?"

I pinched the bridge of my nose in frustration. I was not trying to have this conversation right now. It was easy to avoid Pops because I didn't have to see him every day, but she had a way of being pushy.

"You are really trying my patience, Connie!" I banged my hand on my desk for emphasis. She looked at me like I was crazy, but didn't move an inch.

"If you have something to say then I suggest you go ahead and say it, son."

"You ain't ready to hear what I got say. I would appreciate if you would just go on somewhere. I'm trying to be respectful."

She didn't budge, but instead stared me down with the same blue/grey eyes that mirrored my own. She was more than a little intimidating standing there in a black asymmetric Tom Ford dress with matching black ankle boots, glaring at me. I had hoped I could avoid this conversation, but she left me with no choice.

"Let me just start from the beginning then. You come back in my life when I'm a grown ass man, after being gone my whole childhood." I placed my index finger on my temple. "Wait, let me go back because you was around for Pops, just not for me. Then you and that nigga make a decision about my life without asking my opinion on it. I don't give a fuck about what y'all got goin' on or how you tried to redeem yourself by keeping me from being a teenage father because you didn't handle your responsibilities as a mother, but both of y'all fucked up my life! What else are you hiding from me? You realize my wife is leavin' me off the back of this shit? I got a daughter whose first steps and first words I missed out on. What else you want me to say?"

She stood there absorbing everything I had to say, and for the first time since I met her, she showed a little emotion. Her usual mean mug softened a little as she bit her lip slightly.

"I guess I deserved that. You have been waiting to say that to me for a few years, so what better time than now? I can't take back anything that I have done, but what I can do is stay out of your way from here on out. You are a grown man with your own family and your own issues, and you don't need me interfering any more than I already have. I cannot speak for Dorian, but as for me, I am truly sorry."

She left quietly, not giving me a chance to say anything else. I felt like shit for the way I had talked to her, but I meant everything I said. My whole life was crumbling because of the shit her and Pops had pulled.

I had noticed that Marissa was getting a little too damn comfortable in my house, but I had mercy on her because of that baby. If me and Mona got a divorce, she was about to be out on her ass.

KNOCK KNOCK.

"Come on in."

My father-in-law walked in the door smiling. "This is a real nice place you got here, son. It looks even better than the last time I was in here."

"Thanks, Pops. What brings you up this way?" He closed the door behind himself before taking a seat across from me.

"Me and you always been able to talk as men, right?" I nodded my head yes. "Because of that, I am going to come to you like I would want my father-in-law to come to me. This situation with you and my daughter has gotten up under my skin. She wouldn't tell me what the deal was so I spoke to your mother about it." That remark drew a frown from me. "I now you don't like people in your business, and I usually make it a habit to stay out of it, but I am worried. I can't get Mona to eat and she hasn't been sleeping either. She is carrying my grandchildren and I—"

"I don't want anything to happen to my children either but she won't hear me out. I have tried everything short of begging her and I'm not gonna do that. This whole thing is not my fault, but she won't get out of her feelings long enough to see that. What am I supposed to do?"

He shifted in his chair, crossing his legs. "I can't tell you what to do or how to feel because you have every right to be mad. I will tell you of a quote I once heard somewhere. I am human so nothing human can ever be alien to me. It means that people make fucked up decisions sometimes, but they are human. Why are we always surprised when people do messed up stuff if we are all human? You can stay mad at your parents forever, but that won't change the fact that you have a daughter who needs you. I fucked up my daughter's life because she didn't come out of my nut sack. Now she won't even call me daddy, and I have barely seen my granddaughter. I have a garage full of gifts that were returned to me because she didn't want my help."

"I am not the one you need to talk to, Pops. No disrespect, but your daughter is the one prolonging this whole separation. I been trying to get her to understand that I'm stuck between a rock and a hard place, and—"

"You didn't seem to be too stuck when you went to that restaurant. I saw the little video along with millions of other people. I'm not gonna speculate about what was goin' on right there, but it just looks bad." He clasped his hands together on his lap. "I didn't come down here to judge nobody because I have enough skeletons in my own closet. I just came down here to let you know that no matter how tough she is being, Mona really misses you. To be honest, she is actually messing up my flow a little bit too." A grin crept along his face until it burst into a full scale smile. "I been seeing this lady for a little while now, and I'm not really ready for her to meet my children yet."

I reached over the desk and dapped him up. "I feel you, Pops. She just got to decide she loves me enough to come back home because I can't beg her no more."

He picked up the picture of me and Mona that I kept on my desk. "I had my reservations 'bout y'all getting married, and you know I never made no bones about that. But what I don't want to see between y'all is what happened with me and Jill. If the bad outweighs the good then y'all may need to take a break. I will say this though, when a woman gets pregnant, her emotions go through some craziness."

I shook my head, agreeing with him. Sometimes I felt like the worst the thing I ever did was get her pregnant.

"I want to see y'all make it but not at the sacrifice of either one's happiness. I feel like I overstepped my boundaries when I came and got her, and as a man, I apologize for that."

"Pops, that ain't your fault completely. If my daughter called me for whatever reason, I'm coming off top."

He stood up to stretch. "I gotta get out of here, but it was good seein' you, son. And whatever happens, you're still family to me. I know you live in that big ass castle, but you can still come back and pick me up or let me drive that automobile or sumn," he joked.

"Man, you can come pick it up any day of the week. I appreciate you stopping by... I needed that."

He shook my hand, noting my pained expression. "You gotta let that stuff go with your parents. They messed up, by they had good reason." He pulled me into a quick hug before patting my shoulder.

When the door closed behind him I plopped back down into my chair. He had kept it one hundred and didn't pick sides like most fathers would have. I sent up a quick prayer before getting back to work. I needed my family back, but we don't always get what we want, now do we?

## CONSTANTINA

The single plait that hung down her back swung wildly as she ran around the playground. "She looks just like her father did. I should have brought baby pictures."

"Yeah, I would have liked to see those." Sitting at the picnic table across from Dannity, I felt remorse that I couldn't hide. "You know it was not easy for me to do what I did because I missed out on my own son's childhood."

She searched my eyes for sincerity and I never wavered. It was important that I gain her trust.

"I can blame everybody for what happened, but I still had the ability to reach out before I did. I guess it was okay for me to allow her to think my gay best friend was her father. I think she picked up on it when he started borrowing my handbags."

I chuckled. "Children are very smart, Dannity. I always wondered if my son had any idea that his mother was the woman pretending to just be a good friend of his aunt. I guess there was no maternal attraction because he was told so many terrible things about me."

She rubbed her palms on her jeans. "What's done is done now. I embarrassed the hell out of myself, but I should have known that he would move on. I mean, he is gorgeous and he has a big heart. What woman wouldn't want a man like that?"

I nervously twisted diamond band on my ring finger. "I spent my whole life trying to find a man to replace his father. I traveled all over the world and was adored by many men, but none of them came close to Dorian. No one in the world knows better than myself how it feels to sacrifice love for family." I held my hand up. "I waited my whole life for this ring. I am over forty, and just now getting to be with the love of my life. I am worried about how Delano will take the news. If he will feel betrayed because I waited until he is grown to do what I should have done before he was born."

She gave me a small smile as Delainey ran up to the table and grabbed her around the waist. "Mama, I missed you. Who is this? She is pretty."

I gave her a small wave, which she graciously returned. Dannity looked up, searching my face for an explanation.

"Hi Delainey."

She placed her hands on her small hips and cocked her head to the side. "How you know my name?" I cleared my throat, feeling slightly embarrassed.

"I am your dad's mother."

Her eyes lit up with excitement as she ran over to my side of the picnic table. "You are my Granny!" she squealed, hugging me tightly.

I hugged her back as Dannity looked on, trying to control her emotions every bit as hard as I was trying to control mine.

"You are white though," she observed, pulling away.

"I am Italian, bambina, and you are too."

"Hey, that's not my name," she pouted playfully. I pulled her into my lap and kissed the top of her head. "That will be my name for you. Is that okay?"

She nodded her head yes. A little girl with a hoola hoop called her name. She gave me one more quick squeeze before darting across the playground.

"She is a mess ain't she?"

I tried to answer Dannity, but felt myself getting choked up. She grabbed my hand rubbing it softly. I felt so conflicted being here with her when I knew Mona was upset with me. I had every intention of meeting up with her to threaten her about revealing herself, but my eyes melted the moment my driver opened the door and I saw Delainey running around in her denim romper and pink sneakers.

"She is the most beautiful thing I have ever laid eyes on." For the first time in my life I regretted the decision I had made long ago. This web I had weaved had entangled the hearts of too many people.

"Dannity, I want to be in her life. I cannot speak for the way this will turn out, but I want her to know who I am. My daughter-in-law is entitled to feel the way that she does about her, but I want to be around."

She took a deep breath as if thinking. "You will be the only grandparent she has. My parents decided that she didn't deserve to have them in her life. I was thinking about leaving here and going back to North Carolina, but I want her to know her daddy, and now that I have your support, I intend to stay here."

"If you need anything, you don't hesitate to call me."

"Yes ma'am, I will. Thank you for everything." She gave me a quick hug.

I watched as she ran out to the playground chasing Delainey. Those were the moments I had missed with my own child, but nothing would keep me from experiencing them with my granddaughter.

# CHAPTER 14

## MONA-LISA (A FEW WEEKS LATER)

I was beyond bored sitting in the house every day. Besides trips to the doctor's office, my life consisted of watching cable and trolling social media. I wanted to go home so bad and lay in the bed with my husband. He had come by a few times, but I refused to see him. As stubborn as I was being, I actually felt the opposite. I just felt the need to punish him, especially after seeing pictures of him and his daughter on his Instagram page. It seemed like everybody was moving forward except for me. Marissa was bitter about Tay, but even she had managed to find a decent paying job, and therefore had no time for me.

I begged her to watch the baby but she always had some excuse. Leslie was not welcome over here, so we restricted our relationship to phone calls unless Daddy was gone to work. I had a feeling I was wearing out my welcome with him because he had asked me more than once when I was going home. I threw the remote down on the bed and grabbed my blinking phone. I was disappointed to see nothing but notifications from Facebook. Going to my page, I saw that Leslie had uploaded a new picture. I looked through my other notifications before going to hers.

My mouth dropped when I saw picture after picture of the inside of my house. She had even taken pictures inside my closet. I had no idea what she was on, and I was definitely about to call her and ask her when I felt a warm liquid saturating the sheets up under me. *I know I didn't just piss on myself.*

Raising up, I looked down at the bed and quickly realized what had just happened. Frantically, I grabbed my phone to call my daddy.

DELANO

"You can sit all of those highballs over here and I'll take the shot glasses," I directed Phillip. I was tired as hell but my specialized glasses for the club with the Motivations logo had finally come in. Normally Constantina handled this, but I still hadn't had too much kick it for her, so I did it myself, even though I had hosted a party that didn't end until a few hours ago. My phone was going off like crazy, but I was determined not to stop working until I was finished. Throwing myself into work had been the only thing keeping me together, except for Delainey.

Phillip stopped stocking the shelves when the bar phone rang. "You want me to answer that boss? It might be the people calling back about the plumbing."

Grabbing a beverage napkin off of the bar, I wiped my forehead. "Yeah, but hurry up, I'm tired as hell," I replied.

As soon as he answered the phone, he looked up at me. "Okay, I will definitely let him know. Thank you so much."

He disconnected the call and ran over, lifting my off of my feet in a bear hug.

"The hell wrong with you?" I laughed, pushing him away.

"Man, get on out of here and help your wife bring them babies in the world."

I snatched him up by his collar. "Don't fuck with me like that."

"Man, that was your father-in-law. He say Mona bout to have them babies, so unless—"

I didn't even stick around to hear what he had to say. Instead, I ran out to my car in such a rush that I didn't even ask what hospital she was in. My phone rang as soon as I hit the freeway.

"I thought you may wanna know what hospital she was in, boss."

"Yeah, that would be helpful," I replied, laughing."

I started sweating bullets, not really knowing what to do with myself. I was excited on one hand but on the other hand I was disgusted. We were bringing two innocent lives into this bullshit we had going on. They deserved to be brought into a loving environment, not this chaos that had become me and Mona.

# CHAPTER 15

MARISSA

I was glad that Delano had showed up so I wouldn't have to. I had no intention on being in a funky ass delivery room. I would much rather wait until she had the babies and they were cleaned off before I came up there. Besides, I had a meeting to attend. I had run into my old friend Sienna from high school and she told me that she had a quick way to make some easy money, so you know I was all ears. For a few weeks she had been telling me about this little escort service her cousin Tahj ran. I wasn't with it at first because I was not about to go back to that life of sleeping around, but when I saw her two-bedroom townhouse in Centennial Park North, I was mesmerized. Her complex boasted an onsite gym and swimming pool with a cute little park that was immaculately kept.

"I know you have a little girl and all, but don't you want to be able to provide for her? I mean, it has to suck living with your sister and her husband."

I gave her a knowing look before taking another sip of my mimosa. "I hate not having my own, but what I hate even more is not being able to take care of my daughter. I don't want to keep working these nickel and dime ass jobs because I want the best for her." My statement was partially true because I wanted the best for me too.

Sienna crossed her flawless legs and shook up the ice in her glass of vodka. "I made five racks last week, and not once did I have to do anything sexually that I didn't want to do. I think that you can do this until you find something else. After my parents cut me off because of my choice in men, I had no option but to get out on my own and do it up. Everything in here is mine, and if a man come in here, he can't take nothing but the bag of rags he came with."

As I looked around at the stainless steel appliances, granite countertop, and expensive artwork adorning her apartment, I couldn't help but to be a little envious.

"So what exactly do I have to do? I don't want to go back to sleeping around because that's how I got her to begin with, I pointed to Tavonda who was sound asleep in her car seat. Don't get me wrong, I love my baby, but I wish I had waited on her. She deserves to have both of her parents."

She took a long sip of vodka before pouring another glass. "I feel you, but just think about what you can get her. I would love to tell you that you want have to get down for the crown every now and then, but I would be lying. Most of our clients just want somebody to show off when they go these ritzy ass conferences and conventions. We even have single pastors on our roster who don't want to make it known that they are gay, so they pay top dollar for respectable looking girls."

I wrinkled my nose up because that sounded a little trifling to me. The way I felt right now I was willing to do whatever I needed to do to get on my feet. Since it was curtains for me getting back with Tay, and Todd was crazy, I had to do what I had to do. My first mind was telling me no, but my pockets were telling me yes. Why don't I ever just follow my first mind?

## MONA-LISA

I didn't know how to feel when Delano walked into the room. He closed the door quietly behind himself and I sat stark still, trying my best not to appear too excited. He walked over to the bed slowly with one hand behind his back.

"How you feelin' Mama?" he asked.

"I feel okay, I'm just a little sore. I fell before Daddy got there to pick me up."

He handed me the small bouquet he had behind his back. "Why didn't you call me? I would have come, no matter what. You could have hurt yourself."

I sat the bouquet down, afraid to meet his eyes. I didn't call him out of spite, but I couldn't tell him that.

"I don't want you to ever feel alone in this, Mona. Regardless of all the bullshit, you still are my wife."

I nodded that I understood as he took my hand into his. We looked up as the door knob turned.

"Damn, you ain't had my grand babies yet?" Daddy joked.

The cup of coffee in his hand smelled like heaven, but I knew I couldn't have any.

"What up, Pops. I'm glad they didn't come yet because I didn't want to miss a moment," Delano stated, shaking his hand.

"I don't want to see none of the pushin' out or nothing because I have not seen my child naked since she was a baby," Daddy joked. "Your mother said she would try to make it to town, but you know how that goes."

I didn't want to see her, so that was good news for me. I couldn't deal with her shenanigans today.

"So, I hope that y'all are reconciling because I love my daughter, but she needs to go home and bug her husband."

We both looked over at Daddy and laughed, but he was dead serious. I knew I was getting on his nerves with my constant moping and rearranging stuff. I was looking forward to going back to my own house, especially since I didn't trust my sister.

"I will be glad for her to come home. I'm tired of sleeping in a king by myself, plus I'm tired of your other daughter," Delano confessed.

We all laughed, knowing what a handful Marissa was. I laughed a little too hard because my stomach began to bother me. I grabbed it, hoping the pain would subside as Daddy and Delano continued to make small talk, but for some reason, it didn't let up. A piercing pain shot through my stomach and around to my back. They were so busy talking that nobody noticed the agony I was in.

"Del, please... get... the... doctor," I whispered as the pain continued to slice through my abdomen like a scalpel.

"You don't look too good, baby girl, are you alright?"

I saw Delano run out of the room and heard Daddy talking to me, but I couldn't respond. I had always heard that pregnancy was a pass over death, and now I believed it. With each growing pain, I could feel myself being ripped away from my body.

*What is happening to me? Please don't take me now, my babies need me. I am sorry for everything I've done, but please don't take me. I know I've been stubborn, but I was really hurt. I love my husband. Please don't take me away.* It seemed like the more I begged for forgiveness, the worse I got. The hardest part was not being able to verbalize anything to Delano, who stood by helpless until the doctors pushed him and Daddy out of the room to work on me.

## DELANO

I had never heard of dystocia. They tried to give me some quick explanation about having to reposition the babies because they were stuck. I thought that all women took hours to have babies, but the nurse explained that Mona was probably much further into the process than she realized when she got here. The only thing I knew was that I was terrified about the idea of anything happening to her or my children, especially since we hadn't officially made up.

The fact that I had to wait outside made me even more antsy. I started to bust up in there, but I didn't want to compromise anything they had going on. I didn't realize how hard I had been pacing until my father-in-law tapped the chair next to him. I sat down reluctantly, but continued to stare at her door.

"You need to be praying instead of worrying, son. I know you love her, but all you can do right now is pray for her. I am not in the least bit worried because I know she will be okay." He patted my shoulder before walking down the hall and pulling out his phone.

I assumed he was calling her mother, so I humbled myself and called mine. As I listened to the phone ring, I silently prayed that she wouldn't pick up and I could just leave her a voicemail, but that wasn't the case.

"Hello Delano," she answered in a very business-like tone.

I couldn't even fix the words to say back to her. I just cried into the phone.

"Delano? Hello? What is wrong son? Hello?"

I handed the phone to Mr. Middleton who had walked back up and placed a hand on my shoulder. He rubbed my shoulder and began to relay the issue to her.

I buried my face in my hands, feeling more helpless than I ever had in my entire life. The moment I had been waiting for all this time had officially turned into the moment that would change my life permanently.

# CHAPTER 16

MARISSA

I cringed as I looked at myself in the full length mirror. The more I thought about it the more I felt like I was making a huge mistake. Leaving my baby with some girl I barely knew was mistake number one, but because of how jealous I was of Tay's friend, I refused to leave her with him. And I couldn't chance leaving her with Petey.

"Girl, you look good. Why are you looking so sad?"

I turned to where Sienna stood in the doorway. She wore the royal blue, backless Valentino gown like it was a dress from *Rainbow*. I, on the other hand, was very careful with the way I accessorized the silver and white Pucci mini-dress with matching silver pumps. The earrings in my ears were dangly five karats and were more expensive than anything I ever thought about owning. The image in the mirror did not belong to me. I didn't recognize the older woman that I appeared as. For a few moments, I wanted to slink back into childhood and not go through with this, but it was no longer an option.

"Here, I can tell you need to loosen up."

I didn't think twice before swigging the glass of champagne that she gave me. I needed something to clear my head fast. She smiled slyly before walking into the living room to grab our clutches.

"You have to be extra careful because all of this stuff is borrowed, and my cousin's neck is on the line if anything gets messed up. Hold that thought," she shushed me as she answered her phone. "Yes, we are ready. We will be right down." She dropped her phone into her clutch. "They are here, so let's get this money, girl."

I took a deep breath and patted my curls gently as I followed her out the door. Once it was locked, she looped her arm through mine and pulled me along as if she knew that I was ready to run. The seven inch heels I wore barely prevented walking, let alone running.

I was pleasantly surprised to see that a white Navigator limousine was waiting on us. The female chauffeur complimented our dresses as she helped us into the car. Sienna wasn't impressed, but I was taken aback by the televisions, mirrored ceiling, and bar. She wasted no time fixing drinks while I pushed various buttons.

"You get to travel like this all of the time?" I asked amazed.

She shrugged as she sipped from her glass. "Personally, I prefer to ride in something a little classier but I guess this will do." She drained her champagne before quickly pouring another glass.

I started to say something to her about it, but I was nobody's mother so I kept my mouth shut.

"I should warn you that we are going out with some assholes, so if they say something offensive don't take it personal."

I sat back in my seat boring into her with my eyes. What do you mean assholes?"

She licked the rim of her glass before answering me. "They may or not be a little racist, but they mean well."

"The fuck you mean racist? What you got me walking into?" An abrupt stop caused her to damn near tip over with her tipsy ass.

"Sorry about that, ladies, they are doing construction," the driver explained as she let down the divider.

Part of me wanted to exit the vehicle at that moment, but because of my greed, I stayed. By the time we got to our location, Sienna had gone through a bottle and a half, but surprisingly she was able to fix her makeup and walk into the mansion like she owned the place. I quickly assessed the occupants of the front foyer, and no one in there was close to being my complexion. I had been had, and to make matters worse, the limo had disappeared as quickly as it had arrived.

TAY

I was so excited for Delano and sad for him at the same time. I could not imagine how he was feeling with two daughters who were perfectly healthy and a wife fighting for her life. The whole situation really made me think about my son and Tavonda. Ever since I had shown up to the house with Raven, Marissa had been acting funny about me seeing Tavonda. In reality it was a bad choice, but she still had never said anything about Petey being up at the hospital. On top of everything else on my mind, I had to turn in the key to this apartment today unless I was willing to pay another month of rent.

I was worried about Raven because she basically had nowhere to go if I let this place go. Her sister from NYC still had not answered her phone, and I started wondering if the whole thing was just something she had made up. It was something about her that made me feel like I needed to protect her, but I couldn't really put my finger on it. She was just so much more respectful than Marissa, which surprised me because of her occupation.

"What are you over there thinking about so hard?" Raven asked.

I turned to where she was snuggled under the covers. "Nothing too much," I lied. She sat straight up, resting her back against the wall. "It must be pretty bad because you can't even give me a straight face. If you are thinking about what I think you are thinking about then don't trip because I paid the landlord last night."

I snapped my head around, facing her. "What do you mean you paid him?" She stretched her arms up in the air. "When you went to grab us a bite to eat he came over here trying to see what you were gonna do, so I paid him. I been laying my head here too, so it was the right thing to do."

"You didn't have to do that, Raven. I thought you were going to NYC anyway." She started twisting one of her dreads nervously. "I called my sister and she said that Grant showed up to her house. I can't go up there now."

The fear in her eyes cut right through me. Whoever this nigga was, he had done some real damage to her.

"So what are you gonna do? You trying to stay here?" I asked, looking around the apartment that was just decent enough to lay your head in.

"I can't go to Ohio, and now I can't go to NYC. I am not trying to be a burden on you, though. Maybe we could get the lease switched over to my name."

I scratched my chin thoughtfully. "Nah, if dude is stalkin' like that, then he's liable to be tracing anything attached to your name. I guess you can stay here until you figure out your next move."

She smiled and grabbed me into her arms. As she laid her head on my shoulder, I felt like she laid her burdens on me as well.

# CHAPTER 17

DELANO

Constantina held my hand as I walked over to the nursery. I didn't want to even hold the twins due to the way I felt. Mona was fighting for her life and a dark cloud had settled over my spirits. They would not allow me to see her, which further killed my attitude.

"You sure you don't want to hold them, son?"

I looked at her, warning her not to ask me such a question again. She took the hint and walked to the end of the hallway where Mr. Middleton was standing. He looked out the window to hide his tears, but his sniffling gave him away. He had called his ex-wife and

Marissa, but neither answered. I figured Jill was still on her way, but Marissa's tacky ass was liable to be anywhere. I shook the thought out of my mind as I stared at Monacco and Duchess. I stuck with the last names we had discussed since Mona had changed her mind a million times. Both of my babies had a head full of curls, although Duchess's were the same dirty blonde as her mother.

I patted the hand that rested on my shoulder." I think you need to at least touch one of your babies. We have to prepare ourselves for whatever may happen." I turned to my father-in-law and hugged him tightly while Constantina looked on.

"I came as soon as I heard, son."

I looked up to find Pops walking up with his hat in his hand. I released Mr. Middleton only to walk into my father's arms. Constantina looked left out but I couldn't worry about her feelings right now. She had no idea what being a parent felt like for real anyway.

"Excuse me. I don't mean to interrupt, but may I please speak with the husband."

I let go of Pop and wiped my eyes as the small. Indian doctor approached me. I couldn't read her face so I braced myself for the worst.

"No worries, Mr. Dawson, she will be okay. Your wife suffered some hemorrhaging so we have to keep her, but other than that, she will be fine. We have her sedated right now, but you may go inside and visit. I ask that you keep accompaniment to a minimum, please."

"I think you need some time with her by yourself, son. We will wait out here."

I was so grateful to my father-in-law that he understood that I just needed a moment alone. I pushed the door in slowly. Mona had tubes coming from every direction and was a bit pale, but she still looked like herself. I kissed her forehead, which was ice cold, before pulling up a seat next to her. I rubbed the back of her hand before kissing it and placing it against my face.

"It's crazy how we take things for granted. I was so busy being stubborn and stupid that I didn't realize you could have been taken away from me. No matter how mad you made me, I was supposed to be there with you when your water broke. How did we fall off like this? I just want to do whatever I need to do to make things right because you deserve that. We gotta put this past shit behind us because I can't change nothing. We have two babies that need us, and for the first time, I'm realizing that I need you." She stirred in the bed slightly, which I hoped meant that she heard me.

I kissed her hand before walking to the door to let my father-in-law come in. I stepped into the hallway but my parents were nowhere to be seen. I walked over to the waiting room and pulled out my phone.

I checked my missed calls and surprisingly Dannity had blown me up. I didn't want to talk to her, but the thought of something being wrong with my daughter led me to dial her up. I waited patiently for the phone to ring as I watched Mona's door.

"Hey, Delano."

"What up?" I greeted nonchalantly.

"I need to tell you something, but it's a bit complicated and..." I cut her off with a long sigh. "You may want to listen to what I have to say before you get an attitude," she warned.

I slid down into the uncomfortable seat before stretching out my legs.

"Go ahead and say what you need to say," I instructed.

I didn't really want to hear any bad news after the day I had, but I figured now or never would be the time.

"So you know how I was telling you that I had a sister I never met?" I had no idea what she was talking about because I had never really listened to her that much, but I said yeah just so she would get it over with. "Well, she turned out to be a little messy ass bitch."

I was growing impatient as I wanted to be by my wife's side.

"Dan, what does any of this have to do with me?" I snapped.

"If you would just let me talk then I will get to that part," she huffed. "The girl went through my damn phone and forwarded our texts to her phone." Either I was sleepy or dumb because I was not following her.

"She must know you or your wife some kind of way because why would she do that?"

"What was her name?" I inquired.

"Her name is Leslie, but—"

"Don't even trip, I got it handled." I hung the phone up and walked back over to Mona's room.

Constantina moved away from her bedside when I walked through the door. I smiled, noticing the rosary beads she had placed into Mona's hands. She patted my back before leaving the room. The most important person in my world was lying on a bed in front of me and all I could think about was how much I had failed her.

# CHAPTER 18

MARISSA

I was not feeling going out again tonight. The escort lifestyle was not for me, and I hadn't spent any time with my baby for real. Sienna didn't care about nothing because she didn't have any kids to think about, but I felt a little fucked up about what I was doing. I looked over at my little angel as she slept in her car seat. As much as I hated to do it, I had to call Tay to come get her because I didn't have a babysitter. "Making Love Faces" played as I finished wand curling my hair.

I rolled my eyes hard before answering. "Are you outside?" I asked with an attitude.

"Yeah, but it's cold. I'll come in and get her." Before I could object, Tay had hung up. I tugged on the slinky, purple dress I was wearing. The deep V-neck made my titties appear even bigger than normal and my booty threatened to unzip the zipper that ran down the back of my dress. I had lightly made up my face with some gold eye shadow to match the zipper in my dress and my shoes and some purple lipstick. A nervousness ran over me when the doorbell rang.

Since Valencia was off work today, I had to answer the door. My heels clicked as I walked down the hall. I could make out his silhouette in the side windows of the door, but I was not ready for the sight of him. He smiled up at me wearing a black and white NY fitted on his head with the ear flaps hanging down. The large diamond earrings that sparkled in his ears were something new. His black hoodie and matching joggers fit like they were tailored for him. I couldn't see his shoes, but the gold band indicated they were Giuseppe.

Just as hard as I was staring at him, he was staring at me. "You look nice," he remarked, causing me to break my stare.

"Thank you. You do too. The baby is in the back."

He went to walk through the door but I made no effort to move. He ended up having to brush against me to get past and I can't say I was upset about it. I followed him to the room where he kneeled over the car seat and kissed her forehead.

"You got her dressed cute. Where she get this little giraffe hat from? Her daddy?" I glared at him, not really knowing how to answer that. I was all ready to bend over and buss it open for him until he said that.

"Why would you ask me some shit like that, Tay?" I asked, crossing my arms.

He stood up straight with a smirk on his face. So now you gonna act like that nigga Petey wasn't up at the hospital?"

My face was frozen in a state of shock. "I can explain that. He just popped up to the hospital, Tay. I didn't even want him there. I been hiding from him ever since and—"

"What you mean you been hiding from him? Did he do something to you?" The dark look that crossed Tay's face was unfamiliar to me, as I had never seen him this mad. I didn't know if I should even say anything now.

"He saw her pictures on Facebook and put two and two together. I didn't even know he was coming up there, and then he threatened me—"

"Say no more. I will bring her back in the morning." He grabbed Tavonda's car seat and stormed out of the house.

I didn't have any idea what he was on, but now I was worried about him doing something crazy with my baby in the car. I didn't have time to really contemplate it because Sienna texted saying she was on her way. I checked myself in the mirror before scrambling around to see if I had everything I needed in my purse. I grabbed the pickle jar out of the closet that held my money and snatched out a twenty before putting it back up. I had no idea how bad I would end up needing it before the night was over.

TAY

I decided to take off tonight to spend time with Raven and Tavonda. When we got back to the apartment, I was surprised to see that she was cooking.

"Dang, you got it smelling all Italian and shit. What you got cookin'?" I asked as I wrapped my arms around her waist.

"It's my homemade sauce you are smelling. I am making some manicotti."

"I never had it, but that sauce is lookin' good by its damn self. Let me find out you a chef." She slapped my arm playfully. "Boy, I wish. I thought about going to culinary school, but that was a long time ago." She got that familiar look of sadness in her eyes as she looked out the window. She continued to stir her sauce in her dazed state. *He must have really messed her up.*

"I'm gonna let you get back to cooking. I just need to work on this song."

"You really serious about your music, huh?" she asked, turning to face me.

"Yeah. I mean, it's the only thing that really kept me from being fucked up after I left the streets. I guess it keeps me out of trouble."

She looked impressed. "That's what's up. I do a little poetry, but nothing major. I been to a couple of spoken word joints and recited a few lines."

"Damn, you got a lot of hidden talents. I might need to get you in the studio with me."

She looked up as I reached into the junk drawer next to the stove and grabbed my notebook. Tavonda started crying as soon as I went to sit down my notebook. "I got her. This sauce needs another forty-five minutes, anyway." Raven washed her hands and wiped them on her boy shirts before picking up Tavonda. She stopped crying instantly, which surprised me.

"Aw, pretty baby, you don't have to cry, now do you? I bet you want something to eat, huh?"

Tavonda smiled as Raven rocked her gently in her arms as she made her bottle. It was something so natural about the way she vibed with her. I settled down on the raggedy couch that she had covered with a flowered throw blanket. She had made it look better in a few days than Marissa had ever tried to make it look. I bit the tip of my pen as I wracked my brain trying to think of a hook for the song I had been working on.

"Come save me. Come rescue me from myself. I need a hero. No, I don't want nobody else. Come touch me. Boy keep me all to yourself. You don't treat me like your trophy. You don't put me on a shelf..." Raven sang as she fed Tavonda, and I was blown away. She had a Jazmine Sullivan type of raspy thing going on that was sexy as hell.

"Hold up. You can sing?" She looked at me with an embarrassed grin. "I dabble. I don't have the type of voice to really go anywhere, but I do a lil' bit."

I was thoroughly impressed. "Maybe you can help me work on this song. I'm trying to do this mixtape and this song is holding me up."

She walked back over to the stove and turned down her sauce before sitting next to me. Tavonda was drinking her bottle as her eyes started to roll back sleepily. "I can try to do a little something. I don't know how good I would be though."

I took Tavonda and handed her my notebook. Five minutes later she had completed my song and improved it. "You like it?" She asked curiously as she handed it to me.

"Damn, ma, you did that? I think you need to come in the studio with me." A pained expression etched its way across her face. "I can't go back in there. After dancing at a place, I try not to ever go back. That's why I have traveled so much. People got a bad perception

about dancers. They think we choose this life and..."
Her voice trailed off as a lump formed in her throat.

"What do you mean? You was forced to dance?"
She shook her head yes as a tear scattered down her
cheek.

"Whenever you are ready to tell me, ma."

She nodded her head before going back to her
sauce. I burped Tavonda and laid her on the couch
where I placed a pillow in front of her. I set down my
notebook and walked up behind Raven. "I am sorry
about whatever it is that happened to you, ma."

She leaned back in my arms. "I thought he loved
me. I did what he said I needed to do to be with him
and keep him. How could anybody be so stupid?"

I rubbed her shoulders as they heaved from her
bursting into a full sob. "Why don't you just tell me

what happened? I ain't a counselor, but I understand about having a hard life."

She turned off her sauce and led me to the floor in front of the couch where we had a clear view of Tavonda.

"I have been judged a whole lot already so please just let me get this out okay?" I nodded and she grabbed both of my hands as we sat Indian style facing each other.

"Like I told you, I was dancing already when I met Grant. He hated it and tried his best to make me feel bad about what I was doing. I had told him how bad life had been with my parents and how me and my sister had to leave them. I didn't really have nobody, and my sister wasn't feeling me dancing. Anyway, he started liking the money that came from it when I was able to start buying him exclusive shit. We were invited to all of the hottest parties because of my popularity, and I was in high demand because I traveled all over the state dancing. I had a chance to talk to athletes, rappers, and businessmen, but I chose him over everybody.

"One night he came home drunk as hell. I had just taken a shower and laid down when he came in the room demanding to smell my pussy. 'Grant please get up out of my face with all that. I am tired and I just got in. Plus, you smell like a damn brewery.' I said to him. I pushed him away from me but he yanked me up by my neck. 'You think you slick? You come in here and wash out ya fish box as soon as you get off? Who you been fuckin?' he said. The stench of liquor, weed, and onions gagged me.

"'I swear baby I ...**SLAP!!** "Tell another fuckin lie! I knew from the force of the slap that it would leave a bruise on my dark but delicate skin. "Please don't hit me baby. I swear I was just sweaty from. " **SLAP!!** Sweaty from sliding up and down on some dick! He slammed me so hard that my head made an imprint on the thin wall.

"You think I like being laughed at? Niggas tellin me that my girl got that wet wet! You a hoe and you always been one. No wonder your parents disowned you! How much you make tonight anyway?" I held back the scream burning in my throat as he crossed the small bedroom and grabbed my duffle bag. I had at least 2 stacks in there that I was saving. "Oh okay you made out nice. How many pussy's you have to eat to make this kind of bread?' He slurred nastily. I knew better than to answer so I kept my mouth shut. That night he walked out of the crib with all of my money and he was so convinced that I was tricking that he started putting me on the track a soon as I left work. I have had three STD's but they were all curable thank goodness."

I felt like I had just watched a bad movie. She had truly been through a lot. I gathered her in my arms and let her cry on my chest. Something inside of me felt like I had met her for a reason. Any thought I had of getting back with Marissa disappeared. As I looked at my baby girl and looked down at Raven, I knew I had my new family.

# CHAPTER 19

MARISSA

I downed the apple Crown as fast as I could. It burned like hell, but I needed at least a buzz before I could even imagine going inside the modest two-story brick house. "Sienna, how did I let you talk me into this? We are supposed to be escorts, so why are we at the house?"

She fixed her eyeliner before snapping her compact shut. "You complain so much. They paid extra so that we could pregame a little before the awards show. I wish you would chill out. You are seriously blowing my high."

I wrinkled my nose as she took a quick puff of the loud blunt before popping open her compact again. "These guys are some rappers that want to look good for the local artist award show. so they paid good money to have the best females on their arms. We won't be the only girls, but we will be the sexiest."

I couldn't argue with that because I knew I was killing it. If Sienna wasn't an undercover coke whore, she would look better than she did, but she still was cute enough to be seen. I popped an Altoid and sucked on it nervously before she was finally ready. I didn't like anything about this particular event because for one we had to drive ourselves, and for two, I was not familiar with Grove Park. All I knew was that we were on Cato street. I stepped out of the car first and took a deep breath before walking up the walkway.

"Dammit! I almost broke my heel on these cracks. How could somebody afford escorts who can't even afford landscaping?" Sienna complained.

I rolled my eyes as I walked up the steps and pressed the doorbell. The smell of weed wafted from under the door. *I am not trying to go to an award show local or not smelling like weed.*

A fat dark-skinned, Rick Ross look alike answered the door. He was swagged out in his all white button down with matching slacks and diving loafers. "Come on in, ladies. Y'all smoke?" he asked, offering me a lit blunt.

"She does, but I don't." I fanned my face and walked around him.

The cloud of smoke was so thick you would think Snoop was somewhere in the midst. The only thing I could make out was the cheap Rent-A-Center sectional and glass coffee table that sat on a gold stand. The pictures were all home interior and the cheap plastic flowers screamed Dollar Tree. *Who decorated this place, Costco?* I laughed to myself. A light skinned mess in a burgundy cowl neck jumpsuit flipped a cheap grey weave as I went to sit down next to her. *Please let me make it through the night without whoopin' some ass. Amen.*

Sienna sat down next to me and blew weed straight into my face. A sharp jab with my elbow let her know I was pissed. Loud, poorly recorded rap played as girls grinded on guys in the middle of the floor. *When the hell are we supposed to be leaving?*

As if on cue, the answer to my question walked into the room, and he wasn't dressed to go to an award show. Stopping directly in front of me, was Petey in a wife beater, some baggy jeans, and a pair of Jordan flip flops. Todd's smiling face loomed over his shoulder as I tried to slide back into the couch. I couldn't believe when Sienna slid over to make room for him to snatch me off of the couch and over the coffee table as everybody looked on and laughed. The pain of carpet burn would be the least of my worries as he dragged me through the living room and into the hall before stopping at a bedroom door.

"I got her first. Y'all niggas gotta wait," he asserted before dragging me in the room and closing the door behind us.

DELANO

I tried not to break down as I walked in. Mona looked 100% lifeless. Had it not been for the imprint on her ring finger, I would not have believed it was her.

Constantina gave me a sorrowful look as I approached the bedside. "I can give you some privacy if you would like. I am going to get coffee. Would you like some?"

I shook my head yes and she disappeared quickly. I bent down to kiss Mona's forehead and was grateful that she still felt warm. "Mona, you can stop being dramatic." I tried to muster a laugh, but I knew it was not about to happen. I held her hands in mine and silently prayed for some type of movement, but I got nothing.

"Hey, son. How you holdin' up?"

I turned around to find Pops standing in the doorway with a bouquet of pink roses. He set them down on the side table before grabbing me into a warm embrace. I nearly fell limp in his arms. "Son, she is gonna be alright. Her father is downstairs parking the car, so I think you need to let him have a moment alone with her. Plus, we need to talk."

I didn't want to leave Mona's side, but the truth was that I did feel a little overwhelmed. I kissed her lips before allowing him to lead me down the hallway to the near floor-to-ceiling window that overlooked downtown Atlanta.

"I know that you are mad at me, but—"

I held up my hand, cutting him off. "Pops, I ain't trippin' about that issue right now. I am mad, true enough, but the only person that truly matters to me is lying on that bed down there." I pointed to Mona's room. "I just want her to be alright. Nothing in this world matters if she does not make it. What at am I going to do with twins? "

"You will have help with whatever you need, but quit talking about my daughter-in-law like she is dead. She is heavily sedated, but she is still here with us. You may have to take on a more active role at the house, but that's about it." He patted my shoulder lightly. "None of this happened for no reason. That girl has been carrying those babies and stressing, and this is probably her body reacting to not getting enough rest.

A man can never understand what a woman goes through carrying children."

I had to agree with him on that. She had gotten on my last nerves lately, but I never took into consideration what she was going through.

"I can't stay long. I have to meet with someone and I got another place to go, but I had to see how you were doing, and uh…" His voice trailed off as he looked down at his shoes.

"What is it, Pops?" He wouldn't raise his eyes to meet mine, so I knew something was up. "I don't know how you gonna feel about this, but me and Connie been kinda seein' each other."

He thought the news would surprise me but it didn't. They had never lost that love they had for each other, plus they were never more than a few minutes apart whenever they came around.

"That's good news, right? It seems to me like everything came full circle. I'm not mad about that." He pretended to wipe sweat from his brow which gave me my first laugh of the day. "Well, my other thing was—"

"Well, well, well, aren't you a sight for sore eyes, Dorian?"

We both followed the voice down the hall to where Jill stood in a dress that she had apparently borrowed from Marissa. It was a denim halter style with cut-out panels on the belly that stopped mid-thigh and was paired with strappy white heels that snaked up her legs. Her hair was shaved on one side with natural curls on the other side. She looked sexy, but in a weird, 'I'm trying to recapture my youth' type of way.

Pops looked over at me and I threw my hands up. "That's all you, pimpin'. I'm about to go check on my wife." I spoke to Jill as I strode past but I side-stepped her attempt to give me a hug.

I took one look at Pops before walking into the room, and I could tell he was terrified. *Constantina gon' kill both of them.*

When I walked in, my father-in-law was talking to my mother. They were both standing around the bed with coffee cups in hand.

"Where are my babies?" a groggy voice asked.

I damn near knocked them over as I rushed over. Mona was lying there looking around with both eyes open. "Hey, Del." She mustered up a small smile.

I cupped her head in my hands and kissed her forehead as I hugged her to my chest.

"Son, you gotta let her breathe a little bit," Mr. Middleton spoke laughing.

I didn't want to let go of her, but I did slowly. Her eyes were a mixture of hazel and green as she smiled up at me.

"Let's give them a moment," Constantina suggested.

Once the door closed behind them, I held Mona's hand up to my cheek. "Ma, you gave me the scare of my life." I tried to compose myself but my voice cracked slightly. "You would have left me in this world knowing that you was still mad at me and..." I couldn't even finish my statement due to the huge lump in my throat.

"Don't cry, baby. I was fighting for you... for my babies. I'm sorry I—"

I placed my finger to her lip. "You don't owe me an apology. I am the one that needs to be apologizing. This whole shit happened because I wasn't honest with you."

"Hold on, bitch, you better get your hand out of my damn face! Jason, you better get ya friend right now before she gets the business end of my red bottom!" The sound of Jill yelling in the hallway caught both of our attention.

"Is that my mama?" Mona questioned.

I shook my head and ran to the door. When I opened it and glanced down the hall, Mr. Middleton was standing in front of my mother and Pops was standing in front of Jill.

"She better go on somewhere because I ain't scared of her. Where ya goons at now, bitch?" Jill continued to yell.

"I do not wish to ever be tacky in a public setting, but you disrespected me. Get ahold of yourself and act like a mother for once in your life." Constantina stated boldly as she flipped her hair over her shoulder. Her light blue eyes cut into Jill like lasers.

"I know *Mommy Dearest* ain't tryin' to talk to nobody about motherhood. At least my children grew up in a house with me!" *Damn that was below the belt.*

"I would address that, but I'm not fluent in ignorance. You want to address me then we can do that outside on the street where you make the bulk of your money," Constantina spat. "Your daughter just had the fight of her life, yet you are out there in the hall looking like a rap video reject in that cheap, denim get-up."

A few snickers came from the nursing station.

"Jill, I think you need to leave. For one, Mona don't need to see you like this, and for two, you have been drinking." Mr. Middleton attempted to grab her arm but she snatched away.

"I had a little nip on the plane, but I'm fine. You in here takin' up for the white girl now?"

"Excuse me, but do we have a problem here?" the security guard asked.

"This despicable, classless excuse for a woman wearing *Payless* shoes is being a disturbance. She needs to leave." Constantina asserted, folding her arms across her chest.

"Connie, let's just leave. Let her stay up here and see Mona," Pops suggested.

"Whatever decision you make, it needs to be quick. This is a hospital not a night club after hours." The female security guard looked us all up and down before turning on her heels. She looked like a low-budget version of Shirley from *What's Happening.*

"We gonna clear out, son, but we'll be back later," Pops said before hugging me.

Constantina kissed me on my cheek before following him to the elevator. I couldn't help but think of how good of a fight that would have been.

"Glad they gone. Take me to my child."

Mr. Middleton shook his head at her antics.

"Before you go anywhere near her, you need to get your mind right. You will act like you have some sense or I will throw your ass out myself."

Jill looked at me like she wanted to swing, but I was dead ass. Mr. Middleton nodded his head at me before leading her to the room. As soon as they were inside, I answered my phone that had been buzzing steadily for the last five minutes. I had missed calls from a number I didn't recognize, and whoever it was had left a voicemail. Assuming it was Dannity, I slid the phone back into my pocket and walked back to the room. Jill and Mr. Middleton were each holding a baby as Mona smiled up at them. I decided to give them a minute and walked into the elevator. As soon as I was inside, my phone vibrated again. This time it was a text from the same unknown number.

**Unknown:** I found this number in her phone under brother.

**Me:** Who is this????

**Unknown:** I tried to call the police

**Me:**?????????

**Unknown:** Marissa is gone!!!

I stepped into the lobby feeling numb. I didn't know what to do or make of the text, so I called the number.

"Hello," answered a whiny voice.

"What you mean she is gone? Who is this?"

The girl began to cry into the phone as she explained to me what happened. Apparently, her and Marissa had been working at her cousin's escort service. They had been hired for a job to attend a local music award show when some nigga snatched Marissa up and dragged her into another room. I knew plenty of local artists, so it was only a matter of time before I found out who it was. Part of me didn't want to get involved with her again, but the other part of me knew that Mona would expect me to. I love Mona too much to let her go through it alone, though. I took a deep breath and made a dreaded phone call to a dreaded person before exiting the hospital.

*This shit is about to get real deep.*

# CHAPTER 20

MONA-LISA

"They are beautiful, Mona-Lisa," Mama cooed as she held Duchess. Her golden curls were the same color as mine while Monacco had his father's coal black curls. They had bright eyes as well. Daddy stood closely behind Mama as she held my baby because he was afraid she would drop her. I could tell from the get up she was wearing that she had to have been drunk when she got dressed. I shook my head and laughed internally. I wanted to ask her about it, but because she was being so nice right now I decided to drop it.

"Mona, you sure made me some beautiful grandchildren. I can't wait to show off their pictures at work," Daddy said as he hugged Monacco closer to his chest.

"I would like to think my husband had something to do with that too," I replied. "Where did he go anyway?"

They both shrugged. "I think he may have went to grab something to eat. I'm sure he's not far," Daddy answered.

I took a sip of the water that was sitting next to my bedside before lying back down. "Grab him for a second, somebody is blowing my damn phone up." I reached up for Monacco as daddy took his call to the hallway.

"I have to give it to you. You did well for yourself, Mona-Lisa."

I thought my eyes would pop out of my head in surprise as Mama sat down next to me, cradling Duchess in her arms. "You have a beautiful home, dedicated husband, and now two of the most beautiful children I have ever laid eyes on."

"I appreciate that."

I was astonished by her continued kindness, and uneasy because I didn't know where it was coming from. I couldn't tell if she was sincere.

"You know something, Mona-Lisa? I made a lot of mistakes with you and Marissa. I never could be with just one man." I didn't want to hear the rest of this conversation but I knew she was not about to stop talking. "I loved Jason, but to me he was not enough of a man. He might talk tough in front of y'all, but he always let me get my way. It was my idea to move to Atlanta to begin with so I urged him to find work here. He left the cleaning service that he inherited to come work down here so I could be closer to Ivory and some man I met off the internet."

"Ma, do we have to have this conversation right now?"

She nodded her head yes so I snapped my mouth shut.

"My point is this. You have a good, strong, successful husband. He ain't pushing a broom or taking out trash, and you are obviously sexually attracted to him. You do whatever you have to do to make it work. You don't force yourself to stay with him for even one day for your children if you no longer love him, though. Don't do what I did. I let the best man I ever had slip between my fingers because he didn't make enough money for me and didn't know how to tell me no. I wanted a rich man who wasn't afraid to put me in my place. I guess you can say I kind of got what I asked for on that end."

I shifted Monacco, who was sleeping peacefully on my chest. "What do you mean you got what you asked for?"

A single tear slid from her eye as she began to rub her face furiously. I thought she had lost her damn mind for a second. After a few seconds of rubbing, an ugly blue bruise began to appear on her pale skin. When she finished, I surveyed the damage. The bruise went down her right temple, over her cheek, and down to her chin. As many times as I envisioned whooping her ass myself, I was horrified.

"Mama, what the hell happened to your face?"

"I got involved with a doctor at the hospital where I work. He was a tall, fine, grey-haired, blue-eyed, white man. Anyway, he started off giving me little compliments, and at the time I was vulnerable. I can admit that. One thing led to another and I ended up going from having lunch at work to having lunch at the rooftop lounge of Ruth's Chris. He was the perfect gentleman." She lowered her head indicating that the difficult part of her story was coming up. "Anyway, I started having over to my apartment, and I asked him why he couldn't spend the night with me. Of course, he was married to a woman he didn't love. He wanted to leave her but claimed she would get everything, so I waited a few months before confronting him. The next thing I know, I ended up with my head through the wall of the women's bathroom at work." She began to cry silently, causing me to tear up as well.

"Mama, he hit you that hard?"

She nodded her head. "I wish I could say that I left then, but he was the one who brought me to your sister's party."

I thought back to that night and how charming he had been. These men really knew how to keep secrets.

"Excuse me, ladies, I don't mean to intrude." My nurse, Jackie, walked in. *Damn, she could have knocked,* I thought to myself. "It's time for me to take the babies."

We regretfully handed over the twins. I watched sadly as she wheeled them out of the door.

Mama took a deep breath before continuing with her speech. "When Jason and I got divorced, I tried to do any and everything low-down that I could think of. I fought him about the house, but didn't try to fight for custody of my children. I trashed him on every social media site I could think of. I even insinuated that he was the one cheating because I couldn't live with what I did. Then I got back online, meeting all kinds of men with money, and this is the fuckin' result." She pointed to her face.

I didn't know what to say because I had never in my life seen my mother be anything close to vulnerable. I didn't even think she knew how.

"Mama, I am so sorry to hear that. I didn't know you had been going through that. I..."

She waved me off. "You were busy with your own life. I don't blame you for not trying to be close to me because I didn't exactly make it easy. I just really don't want—"

The door flew open, scaring the hell out of both of us. The look on Daddy's face was a mixture of sadness and frustration. "Jill, we need to talk right now."

She looked at me panicked as she held her face. "Can it wait? I need to go in the bathroom and freshen up my makeup."

"Girl, ain't no time to do all that. We got a situation and... what the hell happened to your face?" He walked over to her and grabbed her chin in his hand as he closely inspected her face. "Who did this to you?" he questioned.

"Jason, I can handle this. It's no big deal."

"It looks like a big ass deal to me. Anyway, we need to walk out into the hall."

"What's wrong, Daddy?" I asked, raising my bed up.

"Nothing for you to worry your little self about, baby. We will be right back."

He ushered Mama out into the hallway. As soon as the door closed I heard a blood curdling scream and then a loud thud. The squeaking of sneakers and people talking filled the air next. *What the hell just happened?*

MARISSA

Well, well, well. You here with the white bitch sellin' pussy? Where the hell my daughter at? Better yet, why ain't she with you?"

I wanted to answer his questions, but his foot in my chest didn't make that easy. "Oh, you can't talk now? You seemed to be doin a whole lot of mouth movin' lately wit ya hoe ass. Stand up!" He ordered.

He removed his foot and I struggled to my feet as I looked around the dark room for something to hit him with. I didn't have a chance because he snatched me off of my feet and threw me on the bed behind him.

"Take them clothes off!" he barked.

"Please, Petey, you don't have to do this. I will let you see her, but please don't rape me."

He laughed at me as I pleaded with him. "I don't want your high-mileage ass pussy. I got something else planned for you."

I was terrified, not knowing what could possibly be worse than being trapped in this room with him. "You gonna keep on playin'?"

He snatched my dress off with so much force that it ripped off my necklace too, causing rhinestones to fly all over the room. I kicked at him, which was a bad move because he twisted my ankle in his hand before snatching my shoes off. The pain of my swelling ankle brought even more tears to my eyes as he stared down at me.

"If you know what's good for you then you will keep your mouth shut," he warned as he turned his back on me.

Summoning all the strength I had, I leapt from the bed and right to the door. I was thrilled when it opened and I ran right into the living room where everybody was smoking and drinking.

"Help me, please!" I screamed to the room full of people, but nobody made a move to do anything.

I could hear a few snickers, but nobody tried to help. My only option was to run outside naked. I stared at Sienna in shock as she smiled at me from the lap of some random dude who had his dick pulled out.

*She set me up,* I thought to myself as I was pulled backward by my hair. A barrage of fists proceeded to pound me from every direction as I was pulled to the ground. I could feel hair being ripped from my scalp, kicks to my abdomen, and I even heard when my nose was broken courtesy of a Timberland boot. Trying to protect myself, I raised my hands over my head and kicked as hard as I could, but I was no match for the assault. In the midst of being beaten, I could feel something being shoved inside of me. The jagged edges ripped into me and blood seeped down my leg as the broomstick was shoved as far as it could go.

"Since she wanna run, turn her over and get that ass too," I heard Petey say.

I was flipped onto my stomach and kicked in my back repeatedly as something slick entered my asshole. The more I screamed, the further the object went in until I felt it break inside of me.

"Y'all need to chill," I heard Sienna finally chime in. "I didn't bring her here to get killed!"

"Bitch shut up before I stick a candle in your ass!" Todd answered. "Matter fact, get Teena Marie up outta here," he demanded.

I could hear scuffling as I was once again dragged into the room.

\*\*\*\*

The sound of the door opening awoke me from my daze. The house was eerily quiet as Todd approached me. I tried to stir in the bed, but the pain didn't allow me to do too much moving.

"Be your lil' ass still," he demanded, sitting on the edge of the bed. "You know why this shit happened to you, right?" he asked, turning his back to me.

I was too afraid to answer, so I kept my mouth shut.

"I asked you a question!!"

"No... what did I do to deserve this?" He turned around to face me with red-rimmed eyes. His chocolate skin and beautiful white teeth were no longer appealing to me. "You ruined my life. I should've killed your ass, but that would be too easy. I been living all these years shot the fuck up. I had to learn how to walk again and do basic ass shit. You got my father locked up and they seized all of our shit! I ain't got nothing, and it's all because of you!! You set me up with Delano. You came up with that weak ass scheme so you could get at me for not wanting you! You was never more than some pussy to me! I loved your sister, but the bitch was too damn weak! Look how the fuck I'm livin' now!"

I followed his eyes as they scanned the room. A huge floor model television sat in the corner with a smaller flat-screen on top of it. There were shoes neatly lined up against the wall and a small loveseat held tons of clothes. This was a far cry from the huge bedroom that he used to sleep in that boasted its own bathroom with double sinks.

"I'm staying from house to house because my mama don't even fuck with me no more. She got her somebody new and moved to Florida, and then you chillin' in a fuckin' mansion when you caused this. You think last night was something? You have no idea what I got in store for you next. You should have thought twice about fuckin wit a white girl you used to tease and look down on in school.

"That nigga Petey better be ready to be a father for real," he snickered as he stood to his feet.

He walked out of the door, slamming it behind him. From the sound of keys jingling I knew he had locked me in. *Lord, please help me. I don't want to leave my daughter. I haven't been the best mother to her but I do love her.* I slowly rose to a sitting position, but the pain in my back and abdomen made it hard to breath, so I slid back down. Observing the dried blood that caused the white sheet to stick to me, I knew that there was no way I would make it out of this with my life.

# CHAPTER 21

TAY

I had been blowing up Marissa's phone all day. It was not surprising that she would pull some shit like this, knowing I had to work. Raven had offered to watch Tavonda but I didn't feel right leaving her there. I trusted her somewhat, but I knew too many horror stories of people harming children that weren't their own.

"Tay, are you sure you don't want me to keep her? I don't mind," Raven asked walking into the bedroom with a plate of eggs and bacon. "Naw, ma, I got lil' mama. I will just take her over my peoples," I lied.

I had texted my baby mama to see if she would watch her, and she eagerly agreed because I promised her a loud pack. I had not been spending enough time with my son anyway, so it would be cool to spend time together as a family.

Raven took Tavonda from me before giving me the plate. "Let me spend some more time with her before she goes since you taking her away from me," she pouted.

I tried not to zero in on the boy shorts that were lodged between her thick ass cheeks. She turned on the TV for me before exiting the room.

"The eggs were sunny-side-up like I liked them and the bacon was just crispy enough, but for some reason, I wasn't that hungry. I set the food on the nightstand and was about to take a piss when "Trial and Error" began to play on my phone.

"Who would be hitting me on the default?" I asked out loud. Most of the people that called me had a specific ringtone, but this was my default tone so I assumed it was a bill collector. I went on to the bathroom and took a piss, but my phone rang a second time. This time, "I Don't Get Tired" played and I knew it was Delano. I grabbed it on the second ring.

"You really need to learn how to answer your phone. You got any strange ass phone calls?" Delano asked with an attitude. I looked at the strange number in my phone and realized I had a text from it a well.

"Yeah, why? What's goin' on?" I asked.

"Give me the number real quick. I'll explain everything in a minute." I repeated the number to him before he abruptly hung up in my face. *The fuck he got goin' on?* I wondered. I checked the text from the unknown caller. As soon as I opened it a horrified scream left my mouth. "Fuck! Who the fuck would... I can't believe this shit!" I could hear the thundering of footsteps as Raven ran toward the door.

"What's wrong, baby?" she questioned.

As she stood there with Tavonda on her hip, I couldn't do anything but collapse at her feet.

"Oh my God. Tay are you okay?" She balanced Tavonda on her hip and slowly lowered herself to the floor with me.

"I'ma kill that bitch ass nigga," I remarked between sobs.

She looked at me with a confused expression. "Kill who?"

I handed her my phone and she dropped it as soon as the picture of Marissa's mutilated body came across the screen. Whatever or whoever had gotten to her had a personal vendetta against her. Her face had been carved like a pumpkin and something had burned her to the point of revealing bone, but oddly enough, it was all on her left side. I quickly got myself together and called Delano back. Apparently he had the number traced. I fuckin love technology because all it took was a Google search.

We were headed to Grove Park to a place I had been to many times. Petey's flunky Mark lived there and we often used to turn up before hitting the studio. I knew the house like the back of my hand. Regardless of how I felt about Marissa, I was not about to turn my back on her. I still had love for her and I definitely felt like she deserved the chance to become the mother that our daughter deserved, and part of me wanted to get at these niggas anyway.

An Hour Later...

I was surprised when Mr. Middleton pulled up to my apartment. I slid in the rental van behind Delano's seat. Nobody uttered a word for at least ten minutes.

"What's the plan?" I inquired nervously.

Delano and Mr. Middleton looked at each other before Mr. Middleton answered, "Why don't you ask that piece of trash behind you. I turned around slowly and glanced over the seat behind me. Petey's badly beaten body was laid across the seat. His mouth was covered in duct tape, but it looked like it was the only thing holding his swollen face together. *They pistol-whipped the fuck out of this nigga,* I thought to myself as I turned back around. I noticed Delano staring back at me through the visor mirror he had pulled down.

"So, I'm guessing he is gonna lead us to Marissa?"

A sick grin flashed across Delano's face as he pulled his ponytail into a bun at the nape of his neck. "We got a two-for-one special because we will get her, and Todd too."

"So Todd is in on this shit?" I was heated now because I knew that this shit was beyond personal.

Todd had blamed Marissa and Mona for everything that happened to him after he got shot. Funny how he ran his mouth to the police about the very same niggas he ended up hanging with in the end. Petey and Mark were both snake ass niggas, which was why I was so outdone with Marissa getting pregnant by him.

"I'm gonna handle his punk ass like his mama should've a long time ago," Mr. Middleton asserted. "Y'all go in there and get my daughter to safety, and leave that muthafucka to me. No offense, Delano, but I won't miss."

Delano looked disappointed but he never uttered a word. Besides Petey bleeding heavily through his nose, the rest of the ride was uneventful. I texted Raven to let her know that I may be home late before turning my phone off.

"Here you go, bruh."

Even though I had my .38 on me I accepted the desert eagle Delano handed me. He got out of the car first, looking around carefully before walking around to the back of the house. It was eerie how quiet the street was for it to be this time of day. Not even a child was in sight. I was starting to think we should have waited until night until the front door opened. Delano walked to the mailbox and opened it casually, signaling for us to come inside. *I know they ain't about to leave this nigga in this car unattended.*

As if reading my mind, Mr. Middleton turned to me, "I got him. Go ahead, I'll be along in a minute.

I slid out of the car casually and walked into the house like I belonged there. The scene I walked in on fucked me up. Shards of glass was all that remained of what used to be a coffee table. There was blood everywhere, and what looked like a crack pipe on top of the TV.

"Where you at, Del?"

"I'm in here, bruh," he answered from the hallway.

I carefully stepped through the glass and made my way to the sound of his voice. He tried to warn me, but the sight of Marissa's near lifeless body damn near brought me to my knees.

"The fuck!" I yelled, running to where she lay limp on a blood soaked mattress. Blood trickled from between her legs. I shuddered as I observed the broken broom handle covered in blood next to the bed.

"I don't think we need to try to move her. Find me a clean sheet to cover her in," Delano directed.

I backpedaled out of the room, almost tripping on the debris in the hallway. He had apparently emptied out trash all over the house. I used my shirt to cover my hand as I opened the doorknob to the hall closet. I grabbed a yellow sheet and ran back into the room.

"Stay right here. I'ma try to clean her face up."

Delano walked into the bathroom and came back with peroxide and a clean wash rag that he used to dab at the numerous cuts on her face. The white foam bubbled up all over as he carefully cleaned her cuts.

"Marissa, where the fuck that nigga at?"

She gave me a blank look and attempted to open swollen lips, but what came out instead of words was blood. "We gotta get her a fuckin ambulance!"

"I got an idea, but you gotta calm the fuck down. Hold her up," Delano instructed.

I went to grab her under her arms but she responded by falling limp. He wrapped the sheet around her naked body as much as possible.

"Okay, you gonna have to take her out the back. If we call an ambulance, that nigga, Todd, gonna run. You gon' sneak her up out of here and get her to the hospital while me and Jason wait for him to come back. He ain't went too far if he left her alive."

I walked to the front door just in time to see Mr. Middleton closing the back door of the van. I indicated for him to come here and explained the plan to him. He handed me the keys and ran inside as I pulled the van to the side of house as close as I could get to the backyard. He had tears in his eyes as he helped me load Marissa into the van as carefully as possible. As soon as I pulled off, my heart began to beat out of my chest.

*Please let me get her some help in time.* I prayed as I weaved seamlessly through traffic.

Meanwhile, Back At The House......

"This shit is a huge ass nightmare. I'm supposed to be able to protect my girls.

"Man, you can't blame this on yourself. You know how hardheaded Marissa is. The girl that hit me said that they were working for an escort service, but I feel like she was set up. The girl just got too much of her mama in her. I just wish I had bodied this nigga a long time ago. Look at this place. Pill bottles, crack pipes, codeine syrup; he lost his mind. I thought after learning how to use his legs again that he would straighten up, but the nigga just kept going."

Mr. Middleton looked out of the kitchen door for the millionth time. "Yeah, but where is he, though?

Where would he hide? Obviously he was coming back to finish his job unless he would have killed her. I bet—" The sound of the living room door opening cut him off.

I held my finger up to my lip as I listened for the door to close.

"I should charge niggas to run a train on her like I used to."

"She would probably like that," A nasally female voice responded. *Sounds like the same bitch from the phone.* "Should I go in there and check on her?" she asked.

"Naw, you need to come here and check on this dick. Her stankin ass ain't goin' nowhere."

"Naw, but you are," Mr. Middleton spoke up, walking in front of me.

With his desert eagle trained on Todd, he looked down at the white girl sitting on his lap. "Get that whore out of here," he told me as he closed in on them.

As black as Todd was, his face had taken a sickly ashen appearance. He looked thirty pounds lighter than when I last saw him. "Bring your ass on," I said to the frightened white girl.

She looked back at Todd before sliding off of his lap. I pointed toward the back and followed her into the kitchen where I made her dumb ass take a seat.

"Are you gonna kill me?" she asked solemnly.

"Ask me another question like that and I just might. Turn your simple ass around, and gone ahead and let me hold that purse and the phone in your bra."

She was surprised I had noticed the phone vibrating against her chest, but I didn't miss anything, The thin fabric gave her dumb ass away. I snatched it from her as I carefully listened to the exchange in the living room.

"You think you just gonna keep on doing shit to my family and live, boy? You have hurt not one, but both of my daughters, and I'm not sparing ya punk ass no more."

I could hear an animated chuckle come from Todd followed by a slow clap. "Yo, do what you gotta do. I ain't got shit to live for because of them bitches."

The sound of two swift gunshots stopped him mid-sentence. I snatched white girl up from the chair and threw her in front of me as we ran into the living room. Mr. Middleton stood over Todd's limp body. I could not believe my eyes. There was no doubt he was gone this time.

"Oh my God, you killed him!" she said, running over to scoop up Todd's head. As the blood leaked from his chest, it got all over her light blue dress.

"You a'ight Pops?" I asked as I cautiously approached him.

It was like his mind was in another world as he stood there staring down at them. I reached for the gun with a gloved hand and grabbed it effortlessly as he walked out the front door. *I knew he wasn't cut for this, but he had insisted on being the one to do it.*

"Why did you do this?" she cried as she continued to cradle Todd.

"Be glad that it wasn't you. You set up your friend, and for what? Some dick?" I asked, bending down to meet her eyes.

"Marissa was  never a friend of mine," she spat. "She used to use me because I had money, but all the while she was always talking about how fat I was. She made high school hell for me, and when I got the opportunity to pay her back, I did."

"What he did to her," I pointed at Todd, "was something that nobody should have to go through. Give me one reason you shouldn't join him."

With that statement she dropped his head on the floor with a thud and attempted to stand up, but I snatched her arm. "Answer my question." I tightened the grip on her arm, causing her to wince in pain.

"I didn't think he would do all of that. I thought he would slap her around a little but..." Tears started to pool from her eyes, but they didn't move me. "I heard her screaming and I knew that it was bad. He never let me see her though. Is she okay?"

"Fine time for you to be worried about that now." I slid my gun back into my holster before shoving Mr. Middleton's gun into her chest. "Grab it," I ordered.

She shook her head no, but I gave her a warning look. Slowly, she took the gun out of my hand. I squeezed her hand as tightly as I could around the handle, just enough to get a good print on it before snatching it away.

"Wh- why did you do that?" she stammered.

"I needed a little insurance that you would keep your mouth shut. For a little more, I took the liberty of taking your license. Go to the dicks if you want to, and you will be explaining why the fuck you left here covered in blood with your prints on this gun. You see where I'm goin' with this, ma?" She nodded her head rapidly. "Is that your car out front?"

"It's my father's car actually. Mine is—"

"Never mind all that. Let me hold the keys." She looked at me fearfully before snatching her purse and handing me the keys to the silver Lexus GS 350. "Take your ass outside and stand by the door. Don't move unless you want to get what he got."

As soon as she followed Mr. Middleton down the stairs. As soon as I heard him pull off I busied myself with the task of calling my clean-up crew. The scene was beginning to discuss me so I began cleaning with the bleach from the laundry room to keep my mind off of everything. I damn near jumped out of my skin when Mr. Middleton got back. This shit bought back memories of murdering Cash and Symphony and that was almost too much for me to handle. I was relieved when the crew showed up almost forty-five minutes later. I quickly peeled out of there realizing I only had limited time to get rid of this car.

"Where are we going?" Mr. Middleton asked.

"I am gonna drop you off at the crib, and then I'ma drive to my car. I already hit Constantina, so she'll take it from there."

He looked uneasy as he nodded his head. He ran his hands over perfectly manicured waves as he contemplated what he had just done. "Delano I just killed a man and I feel nothing. Is this normal? Why don't I feel anything?" he emphasized by pounding his fist on the glove box.

"You don't feel anything because you did what I failed to do. He got what the fuck he deserved, and if that bitch rats then she will get a little bit worse." He shook his head before turning toward the window.

When we pulled up to his house I made sure to park across the street. He looked a wreck in his work jumpsuit and boots, but not out of the ordinary. His face was covered in sweat and pit stains had begun to form under his arms.

"I appreciate you going. I know that Marissa was terrible to you and—"

"I didn't do it for her. Go in and get dressed as fast as you can, and bring me back that jumpsuit and those shoes," I ordered.

He got out of the car and casually strode into the house. Five minutes later he handed me his clothes and I made my way to the club where I left my car. As much as I hated to enlist my mother's help, I knew she lived and died for this type of stuff. I pulled into the parking lot, leaving the car running as I grabbed everything out of the car.

As soon as I walked in, Constantina stopped helping Phillip stack glasses and walked over to me. "Go take a shower, give me those clothes, and lock the guns in your safe."

By the time I had gotten out of the shower I opened the door to see a pair of navy blue slacks, black button-down, and black driving loafers laid out on my couch. She had even bought me new underwear. I dressed hurriedly before walking back to the bar area where she was seated with a glass of wine.

"Sit," she demanded sliding out a chair with her foot. I took a seat, observing the empty wine glass in front of me. "Have some."

I reached out my glass as she poured me half a cup. "Delano, this is my last time saving you." That statement caught me off guard. "What does that mean? Ain't this what you like to do? You fix stuff, right?"

She smiled before taking another sip of her wine. "I came here to try to forge a place in your life. It seems that I have caused more commotion than anything. I guess I foolishly believed that we could have a mother-son relationship. I see now that will never happen. You have too much resentment."

I drained my glass before responding. "It's not that at all. You are a woman, and women like attention. You see all of the attention that I lavish on my wife and it made you wonder why I didn't do the same with you. You been here from me these last few years, but you showed up after I was grown. How do you expect me to welcome you with open arms? I missed out on my own daughter's life because of decisions you and Pops made behind my back. I don't want to sound ungrateful for everything you have done, but it's kind of too little too late for some of this." She looked down at the table and I knew it was only to avoid my eyes. I didn't want to hurt her, but I had bitten my tongue for far too long. "I do want you to be in my children's lives. You would probably be a hell of a grandmother, and I know you would protect them with your life."

Her face lit up as she stared at me with those icy blue eyes. "You mean that? You really want me to stick around?"

"I'm just saying that they deserve to know who their grandparents are. If something ever happens to me or Mona, I know that you would jump in there and take care of them."

"That means so much to me. Now that this tender moment is up, let me get back to the task at hand."

Just that quick, her soft expression had turned dead serious as she stood and grabbed the bottle of wine. She walked over to the bar, handed the bottle to Phillip and made her way to my office. Somehow I felt like she had just suckered me into begging her to stay and I fell for it.

# CHAPTER 22

TAY

Listening to the doctors list of injuries was surreal. Marissa ended up with a perforated colon, concussion, broken nose, two broken ribs, and her vagina was ripped in three places; that was just the short list. It pained me to see her like that. Her silky black hair had been chopped off haphazardly, and the cuts on her face meant she would never look quite the same. The beeping of the heart monitor was the only thing that made this real to me. The worst part was seeing Mona wheeled to her bedside. After all she had been through, the last thing she needed was to see her sister broken up.

There was a knock at the door before Mr. Middleton stuck his head inside. He appeared to have a fresh haircut and had changed into some khaki pants and a white dress shirt.

"Is she sleeping?" he whispered as he carefully closed the door behind him. I nodded yes. He tiptoed in as lightly as he could in the dress shoes to stand on the opposite side of her bed. He rubbed her face gently before kissing her forehead. "He worked my baby over," he whispered.

"Yeah, he did her pretty bad." I was about to say something else when I remembered that I never saw Petey leave the van.

"I got his ass and that other one too."

I was confused because I never saw Petey leave the van. I was so consumed with getting her to the hospital that I had completely forgotten about him. A tight knot began to form in my stomach.

"I left that nigga in the back of the car." I jumped up, but he held his hand out.

"Nah, he ain't in the van. I took care of him while y'all were in the house. He is on a first class descent to hell where he belongs."

Not wanting to know too many more details, I quickly changed the subject. "I need to go check on Tavonda. I will be back later." I shook his hand and headed out the door in time to see Jill coming down the hall. The few encounters I had with her weren't great ones, so I kept it moving and walked the opposite way.

After hopping off of the elevator I called Star and checked on my son. For some reason, Raven, was not answering the phone, which made me very nervous.

*What was I thinking leaving that baby with her?* I tried to ditch the thought, but the truth was I was terrified that she may have done something to my daughter. I called three more times before swerving through traffic like a mad man.

When I pulled up to the apartment I noticed an *Aarons Rental Service* truck double-parked outside. Finding the closest space I could, I hopped out of the car and ran down the court to my apartment. My hands shook as I fumbled for the keys, but when I pressed the door it was wide open.

"Hey baby. I wanted to surprise you., Raven announced as I took in the maroon colored leather sectional with matching recliner and the 64-inch flat screen that sat on a cherry wood entertainment center.

"What is all this? Where is the baby?"

Her dimpled smile fell into blank stare of disappointment. "She is in our new bed sleeping. I thought that…"

I walked straight past her and into the bedroom, which had a beautiful queen sized bed sitting on a stand and matching faux marble armoire and dresser. The floor had even been covered in what appeared to be a very expensive grey and blue rug. I kissed Tavonda on the back of her head and sighed, feeling relieved, when Raven appeared in the doorway.

"You, sir, are an asshole. I come in here and try to make thus dump livable, and all you can do is walk through here like I would harm your child?"

I didn't feel like arguing with her after the day I had, and thankfully I didn't have to because the delivery man knocked on the door to bring in the dinette set, which I was sure we wouldn't have enough room for. I did feel bad because I appreciated everything she was doing, but part of me felt like this was happening way too fast. She needed to pump her brakes just a little bit, and truthfully, after what happened to Marissa, I knew that she would need some extra care. I may even have to bring her over here. A nigga was confused, and right now all I wanted to do was get my mind right. I opened my closet door and stood on my toes to reach to the top shelf where my loud was usually kept.

To my surprise, the bag was bigger than I remembered it being and there was a gallon sized Ziploc bag next to it with some shit that looked like Fruity Pebbles. I had seen it in magazines but I had never messed with it, so I stuck to what I knew. I walked back out of the living room while Raven told the delivery men where she wanted everything at. She had to have spent and arm and a leg on this stuff from the looks of it. It didn't escape me that the delivery man kept looking at her ass. I would have to check him about that later, but for now I was about to roll up.

Out of habit, I looked both ways before walking into the car. As soon as I was safely in and set up to smoke my phone rang. *Damn, it never fails.*

"What up, Del?"

"Just callin' to see how you was. You been watching the news?"

The pit of my stomach dropped as he asked that. I hadn't thought to look at the news. "Nah, I haven't seen it. What's goin on?"

"Nuthin' much I was just seein' if you heard anything yet. You know bad news travels fast in this city. You good, though?"

"Yeah, I just left her. I'm at the crib now and Raven got my shit laid out like Windsor Castle or some shit. She getting too comfortable, fam."

"Did you come home to your child crying? Did she steal anything?"

I chuckled because I knew where he was going. "Nah, everything was kosher when I got in."

"Well, don't hold her past against her. You are focusing on what type of chick you thought she was. All dancers ain't hoes."

I contemplated what he said and truthfully all I saw when I looked at her body was how many niggas must have seen it. Not to mention the extra shit her ex made her do.

"I know that you feelin' some type of way right now about Marissa, and I respect that, but you gotta think about long term who is gonna make you happy. I gotta go though, because I'm about to grab Mona something to eat. Make sure you make a decision you can live with."

After disconnecting the call, I leaned back in my seat and contemplated as I smoked.

True enough, me and Marissa had some years invested, but in that time the bad outweighed the good. She didn't really support my dreams and she was always complacent. There were so many times I tried to push her to achieve something, but all she ever did was think I was trying to be her daddy. The fact that she had been escorting showed me that nothing had changed. She hadn't even been a good mother to that precious baby who didn't ask to be here. Don't get it fucked up, though, she didn't deserve what she got, but it was what she was destined to get due to her poor decision making.

After my second blunt, Delano texted me asking if I was coming in to work. I definitely needed the money, so I responded yes before walking back to the house.

"If you would just sign here then I'll be out of your way, ma'am."

I eyed the delivery man as he leaned over Raven while she signed. If he was any closer to her neck, he would have been one of her dreads.

"Damn, fam, you a handwriting analyst?" They both shot me a confused grin. "If you was any closer to her I would think y'all was a couple. Give her fifty feet, my nigga."

He looked at me like he wanted to pop off, but his Craig Mack lookin ass knew what it was.

"Thank you very much for everything," Raven remarked sweetly. I knew she was trying to piss me off.

"Yes ma'am, and if you need anything else, here is my card."

I walked up on him and snatched it. "I got your card, uh... Tyrone. I'll call you if we need anything.

Baby, get the thirsty man a drink for the road," I remarked and patted him on the back.

He marched his ass out of there like a band major while Raven placed her hands on her hips.

"You are a piece of work for real. What is your problem?"

"I had a very rough day, Raven. I'd rather not talk about it, and I'm sorry if I took it out on you." She didn't look too convinced so I grabbed her up, cuffing her booty. "Some shit happened today that I can't talk about and it messed with me. I appreciate everything you did in here. I really wish you hadn't spent so much money, though."

"That's where you're wrong." She giggled. "I got all of this stuff cash-and-carry. Everything is a little bit damaged, but it's still nice. I just want you to have a decent bed to sleep in and a nice recliner to write songs on. You deserve better than this, but this was the best I could do for now."

I tried not to display my emotion, but it was all I could do to keep from getting choked up. She had done more for me than anybody else had ever done. Even with Starkisha, I only got things because she wanted to have something to rub in my face. I tilted her glossed lips up to mine, gently parting them with my tongue. Her kisses tasted like banana candy as our tongues made love to each other. I gripped her ass in both hands as I gently lifted her onto the dining room table.

"Lay back," instructed as I began to pull down her leggings. She was freshly shaved, just the way I liked it and her natural scent wasn't enhanced or masqueraded by body sprays because she didn't need them. I tossed her leggings and panties across the floor before pulling her towards me. "Hold them legs up ma."

She followed my command and held her legs up as I slowly began to blow on her clit. With each blow, she released her legs. "Uh uh, I said. Hold 'em up or I'll do it for you." I blew directly on her clit again, causing her to try to run from me.

Taking both legs in my hands, I pressed down firmly on the back of her thighs, cupping my hands around the backs of her knees before running first my nose then my mouth over her pearl. A small drop of liquid oozed out of her tunnel and I took the liberty to slurp it up, causing her whole body to shiver.

"Mmmm, that feel so good," she moaned.

"Shhhh, before you wake up the baby. Just lay back and take this," I instructed.

Her dreads beat against the side of the table as I parted her lips and slurped the soul out of her. My tongue beat against her pearl like a boxing glove. The more she kicked and screamed, the more I dipped my tongue in and out of her honey pot until I felt the warm splashes of her squirting in my face. She looked slightly embarrassed as she sat up on the table slowly.

"Why you got that look on your face?" I asked, wiping my mouth on my sleeve.

"Damn, nobody ever made me feel like that before. Don't mess around and make me fall for you, Tay, because I don't wanna be hurt." The look in her slanted eyes burned right through me. Hurting her was the last thing I ever wanted to do.

"You don't have to worry about that. I'm not Grant. I am the one who is about to reverse everything that he did to you, but you gotta be patient with me. I never really had a real relationship."

The sound of Tavonda crying broke up our little tender moment, but I wasn't tripping because I knew we would have plenty more of them.

## MONA-LISA

I was distraught at the sight of my sister. Her beautiful hair had been ripped from the roots, her face was slashed up, and she had on a cast that covered nearly half of her body. I didn't know the details and didn't want to. All I wanted to do was go home with my babies and my husband, and go get my niece. Marissa had always gotten herself in bad situations, and to be honest, I was over it right now.

"Knock, knock," Daddy said as he opened the door. He had a huge smile on his face. "How you feelin' baby girl?"

He looked like new money in his navy slacks, black driving loafers, and navy dress shirt. His hair was freshly cut, face trimmed, and I could smell his cologne as he walked up to my bed. I had not seen him look this happy since he divorced Mama.

"The doctor said I get to go home with my babies tomorrow so I'm good. I just hate seeing my sister in here like that. Have you all found out any more about what happened? Marissa has made her fair share of enemies but I still can't imagine why anybody would violate her like that."

Daddy gave me an odd look before biting on the side of his bottom lip. He only ever did that when he was nervous. "I uh... I am going to uh... let the police do their job. I don't think we really should be discussing that right now. Let's talk about something happy." His eyes fell to the floor, which is what set my mind to work. He knew something that he wasn't telling me.

"Hey now."

I glanced up to find mama walking in looking much better than the last time I saw her. Her makeup was a subtle shade of earth tones and she wore a cute khaki cargo dress with matching boots. Her hair was feathered to the side revealing a pair of yellow diamond earrings.

"Hey Mama," I responded scooting up in my bed.

"I hope I didn't interrupt. Jason, you look nice," she commented, eyeballing him.

If Daddy hadn't been a milk chocolate color, he may have just blushed. "So do you, Jill. You look mighty fine today. Mona is going home tomorrow," he announced.

She clasped her hands together dramatically, gazing up to the Heavens. "Thank you, Jesus! I just left Marissa and she is not doing so well today. She saw her face for the first time and she's upset."

I could only imagine how she felt because Marissa was the vainest person I knew. Her ebony skin, long waves, and perfect video vixen body were always a badge of honor to her. Now that she had cuts on her face that had bubbled up, I knew she would be depressed.

"I just wanted to stop by before I go to the airport. I wanted to stay longer, but I have used up my vacation days."

"You leavin' already, Mama?" I was surprised at how panicked my voice sounded. I really did not want her to go.

She walked over to the bed and rubbed my head. "I gotta get back, honey."

I was terrified for her to go back home to that abusive man, but it wasn't my decision. "Just take care of yourself, Ma."

"I will," she whispered before kissing my forehead.

I felt her slip something into my hand before she gave daddy a hug and left the room. He watched her until she disappeared down the hall

"I see you staring, Daddy. Let me find out...."

"Find out what? I still love Jill very much but I can't put myself through that trauma again. Sometimes you have to accept people for who they are, and that means loving them from a distance. I gotta go to work in a few, so I'm gonna be leaving out too. I think Delano said he was coming up here."

I wrinkled my brow in frustration because he hadn't been answering my calls all day.

Daddy kissed me on the cheek before he left me to my thoughts. So much had happened in such a short time, that I was trying to piece everything together. I wondered how life for my sister would ever go back to normal once she left out of here. Helping her with Tavonda was a no-brainer, even though I did want her out of my house.

I hated that she had messed up with Tay, who had been so good to her. *Let me get my mind off of this negative stuff.* Grabbing my remote, I flicked through the channels. I really wanted my babies, but earlier the doctor said that they wanted me to have all of the rest that I could get.

After not finding anything interesting to watch, I decided to hit Leslie up. We hadn't really talked since she spent the night with me. I had never gotten the chance to ask her about the pictures she took inside my house. As I waited for her to answer I flipped over to the news.

"Hi Mona." I had to look at the phone to see who I had called because the voice didn't sound like Leslie at all.

"Hey girl. I had my babies," I informed her cheerfully.

"That's good for you. I guess while you're welcoming life, I am mourning the loss of life. Granny died in her sleep last night."

I almost dropped my phone thinking I heard her wrong. "Oh my God, Les. I am so sorry. Are you okay?"

"I don't know what I'ma do without my granny. Grand-daddy is the one that found her so he's taking it the hardest. He been with her 55 years, Mo."

My heart truly went out to her because these were the only family members that she had. I listened to her crying into the phone, not really knowing how to comfort her. I had never really lost anyone that close to me.

"Les, I am getting out of here tomorrow so you are more than welcome to stop by or call me if you need anything. Keep me aware of the arrangements and I will see what I can do to help."

"I will. I'll probably just inbox or text you because I'm not gonna be up to talk on the phone."

Before we said our good byes I sent up a prayer for Leslie's family. After disconnecting the call with her I called Delano for what seemed like the hundredth time but he still wasn't answering. I was starting to feel some type of way. When I got home tomorrow we were definitely gonna have to sit down and talk.

# CHAPTER 23

DELANO

"So you want to do this now?" I stared down at Dannity in disbelief as she sat in her car with her arms folded firmly across her chest. I glanced in my car at Mona's shrimp fried rice that was getting cold.

"I am tired of the rejection, Delano. You got your little family and there is no room in your life for me and Delainey."

I looked at my sleeping daughter who was sprawled out in the backseat. Her mass of curls was pulled up into a bun with a huge sun flower bow fastened around it. The khaki jumper she wore matched the Sperrys that were on her feet.

"Your problem is that I don't want you. You know I love my daughter, Dan. I have had a lot of shit going on true enough, but do you really think this shit is fair? I mean, what does your boyfriend think about this?"

She smirked at me. "Lawrence ain't hardly my boyfriend. In fact, I been keeping him away from you just so he won't try to flirt. He likes 'em light-skinned." She laughed again, but I wasn't close to being amused. I wanted to yank this door off of her car right now and take my daughter.

I knew that there was nothing I could do at this point to make her change her mind. "Can I at least say goodbye to her?"

She brushed a stray hair from her face. "Make it quick. We need to get back to the house and meet the movers." She popped the lock and I snatched the door open.

"Hey, baby girl," I whispered.

Delainey looked up, wiping the drool from her mouth. "Daddy!" She screamed jumping out of the car and into my arms. I kissed her forehead as she settled her head in the crook of my neck. "Daddy, where you been?" she asked innocently as she pulled away to look in my eyes.

I could feel my heart break in a million pieces as she waited for answers. *If I lose her now, she will always wonder that very thing.* I bit down on my lip to keep from tearing up. "Daddy been busy, baby. You got a new brother and sister and—"

"That's enough time!" Dannity yelled, getting out of the car. "Say bye to your daddy so we can get out of here."

"Mama, he just got here," Delainey whined as she tightened her arms around my neck.

I held her tightly as a tear slid down my cheek. "Dan, you ain't gotta do this," I pleaded.

She threw her hand up, not hearing anything I had to say. "Put my daughter down, Delano."

Not knowing what kind of stunt she would pull, I went to pry Delainey's arms from around my neck.

"No, Daddy! I wanna go with you!"

It killed me to have to sit her down on the ground. She responded by wrapping her arms around my leg.

"See, this is why I should've just left. Bring your ass on, Delainey, before you get a whooping."

Delainey looked up at me, expecting me to protect her. Her beautiful eyes had turned a light shade of blue that I had never seen before as she pleaded with her eyes.

"I see you wanna show out." Dannity snatched her by her arm, ripping her away from me before damn near tossing her in the car.

"Are you out your mind? You don't grab on her like that," I huffed, getting in Dannity's face.

"Seeing as I am the one that raised her, I will do what I damn well please. You ain't nobody but seasonal Daddy any damn way," she spat.

She opened her door and I slammed it shut, pinning her against the car. "This shit happened the way it did because of you. You hid this shit from me. Now you can't get your way, and you think I'm about to let you take my seed? You got another thing coming."

"If you don't move out of my way I will start screaming, and surely somebody will call the police on you."

As bad as I wanted to choke slam her, I just backed up, feeling like a failure as she got in and pulled off. My baby pressed her face against the window, waving as they disappeared down the street. I picked up the first thing I could find, which was a glass liquor bottle and tossed it as hard as I could. I thought it would ease my frustration, but it did nothing of the sort. I suddenly didn't feel like going to the hospital, but I knew I needed to see my wife.

\*\*\*\*

"I am so sorry, baby," Mona spoke as she held Duchess. I cradled Monacco in my arms but the sense of loss was still unreal. "I know how I once felt about the situation, but Del, I am willing to help in any way that I can. You love that baby and she deserves a stable family."

Her words did little to comfort me because I didn't know if they were sincere. I knew how adamant she had been about me not being involved with my daughter in the first place. It was hard to believe she would change her tune that quickly. I felt broken, and to top it off, my phone had been blowing up all day. None of the calls were from Dannity so I ignored them.

"I am gonna have my lawyer to look into it and see what could be done, but I don't have a leg to stand on. It will look like I abandoned my daughter. My parents really fucked me on this one," I spat bitterly. I was tired of being mad at them but I needed somewhere to place the blame right about now.

"Well, whatever we have to do, we will do it together," Mona replied, rubbing my hand.

I smiled for the first time that day. I knew she was serious now, and that gave me a little more hope. We rocked in the chairs with the twins until they drifted off. Tomorrow, she would be going home and we would be doing this all by ourselves. That was a thought that terrified and excited me at the same time, but right now I was consumed. After the nurse came in to get the babies, I kissed Mona and left. I had to clear my head, and her feeling sorry for me wasn't making it easy.

I had just settled into my car when my phone rang. I never liked answering unknown numbers, but this time I made an exception. "Talk to me, I'll listen."

"I bet you will listen now that you got your lil feelings crushed," answered the female voice.

"Dannity?"

"No, this ain't no damn Dannity, but you're getting warmer." I couldn't place the voice for the life of me and wasn't in the mood to play games. "Who is this?"

Laughter filled the phone line. "You don't know who this is? Let me give you a hint. I used to be your wife's bestie."

My jaw instantly clenched. I never liked this bitch. "How did you get my number? Better yet, why are you calling me?"

I killed the engine and waited for a response. "You know I thought it was cute the way you and Mona-Lisa walked off into the sunset while I was left to suffer. After the shit you pulled with Todd, all you got was a slap on the wrist. Meanwhile, I got stuck living with my grandparents while y'all living it up in a mansion."

"How you know where I live at?" I knew the answer would likely piss me off, but I needed the truth.

"Your wifey invited me over. You got a real nice place. It's really too much house for the two of y'all. Yeah, I spent the night and made breakfast in that big ass kitchen. By the way, how is Mona feeling? It seems like she went to the hospital shortly after eating breakfast with me. I hope it wasn't something I slipped into her food."

"Bitch, let me find out..."

"No need for name-calling. I just thought some extra seasonings from my granny's herb collection might make her feel a little better. Anyway, I just got off the phone with my sister. You know, your baby mama? Seems to me that they are moving away, and I wanted to personally rub it in your face."

"You a miserable bitch, you know that? Mona couldn't see I,t but I always saw right through you. A woman like you always meets a bad end."

"Oooh, is that a threat? Talk dirty to me, then." She giggled. "Looks like the only one meeting a bad end is you. Let me get off this phone and watch what—Oh my God!" I almost dropped my phone as I heard the sound of a horn blowing followed by breaking glass.

"Leslie? Hello? Leslie!" The phone line went completely dead as a sorrowful feeling coursed through my veins. From the sounds of it she had been in a car accident. I didn't have any regards for her but I wasn't heartless. "Damn that's fucked up," I mumbled as I dialed the number back. It rang several times and just as I was about to hang up there was an answer.

"Hello?" The voice sounded like that of an older white lady.

"Yes, ma'am, I was just talking to my friend and the phone died," I lied. "Is she okay?"

There was a long pause. "Son, I am afraid there's been a bad accident out here on I-285. There's a few people out here that stopped, but... she was already... there was nothing we can do son. We called the ambulance and somebody is talking with them now."

I could hear the wind blowing as well as a lot of people talking, so it was getting harder to hear her. I pulled up my GPS to see what I could see and sure enough it was where I-285 met with I-75. That was one of the most dangerous stretches of road in the state.

I listened to her try to give me a play-by-play as I frantically drove to the site. It wasn't that I cared so much, but I kept having a funny feeling. By the time I got close, there were cars gridlocked in traffic as the police had several lanes blocked off. I counted eight squad cars as I pulled over onto the emergency lane and got out. It was complete chaos as everybody rubber-necked when they passed through on the one lane left open. My heart sank as I walked what had to be at least a mile and a half to get to the scene. The first thing I saw was a red Denali that was flipped all the way over. The top of the truck was completely caved in, so I knew that whoever was in there had lost their life. The second vehicle was a green Buick Regal a few feet ahead that had veered into the concrete divider causing it to smash the entire driver's side. There was glass and blood everywhere.

"I'm sorry, sir you need to back up," an officer instructed as I approached the scene. I wanted to go further but I heeded his warning.

"Well me and my husband Roy were coming from the doctor and we were just driving along, ya know, when we saw this. It looks like the lady driving the Buick was speeding a little bit and when she got to close to the barrier she tried to switch lanes. Well, the big truck there was already in that lane and when she saw that she tried to get back over by the wall. Well, the person driving the truck just mashed them breaks and before you know it he flipped over. Me and Roy pulled over to the side there in the little white Cavalier and ran over to help. I'm a retired nurse ya know and—it was just awful, Officer."

I eavesdroped on the conversation as I watched the police continue to interview witnesses. The next thing I knew, CBS46 had arrived on the scene. The ambulance doors were already closed, so I had no idea which one she was in. I turned on my heels to leave when I heard something that chilled me to the bone.

"Those poor ladies in that Buick. I can't believe that. I hope neither one of them left behind children."

I felt like my knees would crumble beneath me but I had to ask. "You say there were two ladies?" I asked the older black ladies.

"Yes, honey. Me and my sister saw the whole thing. That one driving the Buick zoomed past us talking on the phone. The other woman looked like she was sleeping," The taller lady answered.

Instantly, I hit Dannity's phone. When it went straight to voicemail I ran all the way back to my car. Not caring if I got pulled over or not, I drove down the emergency lane and hopped off the next exit. I wasn't worried about the police following behind me. The only thing on my mind was finding out where the hell my daughter was.

## THE NEXT DAY

I was a mental wreck. I had called every hospital in Atlanta, and none of them released information to me. I even went by Leslie's grandparents house, but her grandfather was so distressed with his wife dying that he could not even process what had happened to Leslie. I didn't have the number of anybody else in Leslie's family. All I could do was sit and watch the news in my office while everybody partied.

Constantina came in to console me, and even Pops dropped by, but I didn't want to talk to anybody. All I could think of was those baby blue eyes that looked up at mine. Delainey expected me to protect her and I let her mama drive off with her. Why she would get in the car with Leslie was beyond me. Could she have really hated me that damn much that she would risk my child's life.

I had to contemplate all of these things while putting on a happy face because Mona and the twins were coming home today. As happy as I was about that, there was still part of me that ached for my little girl. We had bonded so much. In fact, everything had been much better when I used to sneak out of town to see her. I hated lying to Mona, but the freedom from her spoiled ways was a welcome change for me as I headed to North Carolina. Dannity had acted like she had some sense for the most part, even though she still came on to me at times. I had tried to do the best I could to make everybody happy, and to see it all end like this was too much for me.

As Mona called for the umpteenth time, I silenced my phone. *I'm on my way, damn.* I connected my Bluetooth to the radio to listen to my Spotify app when another call came through. I rubbed my head in frustration before taking the call.

"Talk to me, I'll listen," I muttered in frustration.

"May I speak with a Mr. Delano please?" The white woman sounded very nervous as she spoke my name.

"This is him. Who is this?" I pulled the phone away from my ear, trying to recall where I had seen this number before.

"Mr. Delano, my name is Officer Daria Cunningham and I am with the Atlanta Police Department Zone 4. We have a bit of a situation down here and we were wondering if you could possibly come down to help resolve it."

My heart started beating a mile a minute. Using my analytical mind, I knew it couldn't have anything to do with the murders since I hadn't been contacted by a detective. I was still leery though.

"Mr. Delano, are you there, sir?"

"Yes, ma'am, I am here. Can you tell me what this is regarding?" I could hear her whispering something but couldn't quite make it out. "Sir, we actually would rather you come in. Otherwise, we will have to employ other tactics."

I didn't like the way she worded that at all. "I will be there as soon as possible," I stated nervously before disconnecting the call.

I had an eerie feeling that I would need my lawyer, so I called up Lauren Capperty. She agreed to meet me there immediately. My fate seemed ominous as I pulled up in front of one of the buildings I never wanted to see again.

## MONA-LISA

The frustration turned to anger as I called Delano for the umpteenth time. I was going straight to voicemail. I should have known all that shit he as saying was because he was in his feelings. Here I was expecting to go home as a happy family, and he was nowhere to be seen. I know that he was down about his daughter, but there was nothing that could be done. If Dannity wanted to keep her away, then in all honesty, she had every right. She had raised the little girl after all. He acted like someone had died when he came up here yesterday. I shook the thought away as my nurse came in.

"It looks like you are all ready to go. Do you have a ride to pick you up?" I shook my head no as I fought the urge to cry.

I knew Daddy would come get me, but that was embarrassing. I didn't want him to know that Del had abandoned his family.

"Oh, okay, well take all of the time you need and let me know if I can call you a cab, sweetie."

I mustered a fake smile, but I knew she could see the pain in my eyes. "I think I will try my brother first and then I'll let you know."

As soon as the doors closed behind her I called up Tay.

"Hello."

"Hey, Tay, this is Mona. Are you busy?"

"Not really. I was about to head up to the hospital to see Marissa. You need something?"

I took a deep breath to keep myself calm. "I was discharged about an hour ago and Delano is busy. Can you please take me home?"

"No problem, sis. I will check in on her and then I will be to get you. Is that okay?" I nodded my head like he could see me. "Yeah, that's cool. I will give you gas money when I get to the house because I don't have my wallet on me."

Pssst, you know your money is no good with me. I will be there in about thirty."

I was relieved as we hung up. At least someone still cared about me. Because I had my babies I knew I couldn't go see Marissa, so I called her room. She didn't answer, so I figured she was either sleep or in the bathroom. I needed to talk to someone. I decided to call Leslie to check on her. She didn't answer either, and I knew Mama was probably at work. I felt so alone. I grabbed the remote to see if could find something decent to watch. The only thing good on this time of day was Maury, and I didn't want to hear about anybody denying fatherhood so I turned it back off.

"Let's see what Facebook is talking about," I said to myself.

I had 76 notifications. Most of them were group invites, so I went to my messages. Surprisingly, I had one from Leslie from yesterday afternoon. Because I didn't have the app downloaded to my phone, I was always missing stuff. I assumed she would be telling me about the arrangements for her grandmother, but I noticed that someone else was added to the conversation.

Lesismore: Hey, Mo. I bet you wondering why I messaged you instead of calling. Some things are better left unspoken. I been feeling some type of way for a while now. You got everything that I ever wanted in a man and lifestyle. I had to struggle for everything I got. It's all good though because your shit 'bout to come crashing down. You see I found out that my long lost sister is your husband's lil baby mama. That's cute, ain't it? You thought you was getting a prize but the nigga turned out to be nothing. Then my sister wants to waltz back up in my life like she should have years ago. Granny was the only person that cared about me and now she's gone, so both of y'all bitches are about to suffer like I did.

The message stopped right there as if she hadn't completed her thought. The anger and anguish I felt mixed together as I called her back. I started to leave her a nasty voicemail, but that was not my style. I would much rather cuss her out face-to-face. I had welcomed this bitch into my home, and she had been on her same tricks. Then to find out that Dannity was her sister really made my blood boil. She only came back around so that she could taunt me with that little bit of information. I turned my phone off in frustration and flipped to the news while I waited on Tay. I cringed at the wreckage they showed on the screen.

"That was a pretty bad accident they had yesterday," my nurse said, walking in. "I was two hours late picking up my husband because of that."

I held out my arms so she could take my blood pressure. "That is horrible. I can't imagine that anybody survived that," I commented observing the state of the vehicles.

"Honey, I been doing this for seventeen years and I have seen people survive worse. God is in control. Your pressure is up a little are you okay?"

I was about to answer her when my voice caught in my throat as Leslie and Dannity's pictures appeared across the screen.

"You okay, honey?" she repeated. All I could do was point at the screen.

# CHAPTER 24

MARISSA

"You don't have to stare at me like I'm a monster. I know I looked fucked up."

"You always worried about the wrong thing. I am staring at you because you just survived something so brutal. He could have killed you."

"Tay, without my looks I am dead. My looks are the only thing I had going for me. Now my shit is carved all up and I'm all busted up. They said that I will need at least six months of physical therapy to walk right." Tay held his head down. I wasn't trying to be negative, but I was realistic about the situation. "How will I be able to take care of Tavonda when I will have to go to a rehab facility? How will I even be able to take care of myself? I didn't deserve this shit!!"

Tay walked over to my bed and placed his hand on my arm, but I snatched away, sending a jolt of pain through my body that damn near produced tears. "You really need to calm down, Marissa. Whatever you need me to do I am here."

I had to smirk at that because he was dead serious. "If you were here then why did I have to get in the streets and damn near sell my body to make ends meet? The moment you found out she wasn't your baby, you disowned us. Yeah, you might be playing daddy now, but you sho forgot about us when it counted!"

He placed his hand on his chest in a surprised fashion that I found rather amusing. "So this is my fault? I admit I didn't know how to process it at first, but there is no way you can blame your bad decisions on me. I love that baby and you know that. Why can't you accept that you didn't handle your business? Why you always blaming somebody else?"

I crossed my arms as he continued his tirade. I would let him get his little speech over with before I kicked him out. I had to admit that he was looking kinda good. His face had cleared up a lot, even though he had a little acne scarring still and his face was clean shaven. The white fitted cap sat low on his head and the crisp fitted white tee showed that he had been working out. He had definitely come up.

"Hello? You know the saddest part about all this?" he asked, regaining my attention. "The saddest part is I've been here over fifteen minutes and you haven't even asked where Tavonda is."

"Oh yeah, where my baby at?"

"Really? That's how you ask? You real fucked up. I wonder if I even did the right thing by saving your life. Maybe I should have let you die like the dog you act like. Take care of yourself, and don't trip, I will take of my daughter." He opened the door and strutted down the hall like George Jefferson.

If he got ahold of my baby, I would lose him forever, and I wasn't about to do that without a fight. I called the nurse in to bring the phone closer to my bed. I knew what I would have to do.

TAY

After I got Mona settled in at home, I called Del. It was weird that he hadn't answered me all day. I would be in the studio the rest of the day making sure that the scheduled artists all got their allotted time. When I called Constantina she said she hadn't heard from him either, which really worried me. I dropped Tavonda off with Starkisha and swooped Raven up from the house so she could go to the studio with me.

"You okay, baby?" she asked, laying her head on my shoulder as I drove.

"I got a lot on my mind right now. I'm kinda worried about my nigga."

She lifted her head up and looked at me. "Who?"

"I can't get Del on the phone and he ain't spoke to nobody. I just don't know what to think." In my heart I knew it had to have had something to do with the other day. I knew this shit was gonna come back to haunt us. It would probably be a matter of time before I would be picked up too, along with Mr. Middleton.

"I'm sure he is okay. He's real busy, right?"

I wanted to tell her everything, but my better judgment prevailed. "I'm sure that's what it is. You're probably right."

She smiled up at me before snuggling up to me again.

I didn't believe a word of what I had just said.

ACROSS TOWN

After what seemed like forever, I walked to my car with Lauren following closely behind.

"Delano, I am sorry about your loss. I cannot imagine how you must feel right now."

I was numb as hell to be honest. I could not believe the day's events.

"I appreciate you being here. I will make sure you get paid in the morning."

She held her hand up to stop me. "This one is on me. Consider it part of my pro-bono hours." She gave me a hug before climbing into her tan Bentley.

As much as I wanted to peel out of there, my heavy heart had me moving in what seemed like slow motion. I took a deep breath before opening the passenger side door. "Wake up, baby girl. We 'bout to go home."

Delainey stretched her arms sleepily before stepping out of my arms and into the passenger side. When I got in the car, she already had her seatbelt on which made me smile.

I went to pull off, but she yanked my sleeve. "No, Daddy, you gotta put your seatbelt on. They taught me a song about seat belts at school.

"Oh yeah?" I snickered as I slid the seatbelt across my chest.

She nodded her head. "You wanna hear it?"

"Go ahead, baby. Sing your song." She cleared her throat dramatically before clapping her hands to make a beat. She cut her eyes at me, so I killed the engine and clapped with her.

*You always wear your safety belt and here's the reason why*

*You have to protect yourself and others when you drive*

*If you don't wear your safety belt then something could go wrong*

*Always wear your safety belt and sing the safety song...*

It was so ironic that she would be singing about this right now. I turned my head so she wouldn't see me cry. I was about to call Mona, but as soon as I pulled out my phone Delainey wagged her finger.

"You aren't supposed to text and drive daddy."

I had to laugh at my smart little girl. I don't know what I was gonna do with her lil' bossy ass. As soon as we made it to the first stoplight she pressed her face against the window.

"Daddy, can we pleeeeease get some McDonald's?"

"You can have whatever you like, baby girl."

# 1 YEAR LATER...

"Mama!"

I jumped at the sound of Delainey's voice as I flipped over my steaks.

"What is it, hun?" I yelled back up to her.

"You gotta see this! Hurry up!"

I set my fork down on the sink and ran down the hall to what used to be Marisa's room. We had converted it into a playroom for the twins so I could keep them close by when I cooked. I instantly welled up when I saw Duchess standing on her own two feet clapping her tiny hands. Monacco was busy trying to eat a block, but he had started walking a month ago. Delainey tiptoed behind her, making sure she didn't fall.

"Come here to your mother," I cooed, dropping down to my knees.

My baby walked right into my outstretched arms and it warmed my heart. I gathered her into my arms and squeezed as tightly as I could without hurting her. I noticed Delainey looking a little sad as she stood there.

"Come here, my love," I beckoned her.

She ran up and hugged me too, and not one to be left out, Monacco lazily crawled over. I was so happy because when Delainey first came home she would not leave her daddy's side. There was so much separation anxiety that he sometimes took her to the club with him when he had to do paperwork. I didn't know what to do with the sad little girl who had lost her mother.

It was tragic how cold Leslie had turned out to be. On the day of the crash, right after she left me that nasty message she called up Dannity to talk to her. According to her gay roommate, Lawrence, Leslie had pulled up and asked to take her and Delainey to lunch since they were moving. He was in the middle of braiding Delainey's hair, which was the only reason she avoided the trip. According to evidence obtained by the police, Leslie had texted and called several people, including Todd and left disturbing messages. She had planned all along to kill herself, her sister, and her niece.

The hardest part of the ordeal was having to tell Delainey. The two bodies were so badly mangled that neither could have an open casket funeral. Dannity's family came to the funeral, but for the most part they were cold and stoic. The only person who showed emotion was Lawrence. Delano promised him that he could see Delainey any time since he was so instrumental in helping us get custody of her. The nerve of her grandparents to decide all of a sudden that they cared. Lawrence verified that they had never met Delainey nor done anything for her while Delano came around as soon as he found out about her.

I wish I could say that I was excited about her coming at first, but all I could think about was the fact that I would be primarily responsible for another child. I couldn't have been more wrong. Delano decided that he needed to take a more active role at home so he decided to let Constantina, Pops, and Tay run the club for the most part. Because of all of the issues surrounding the studio, he decided to buy a building to house it in and had off duty officers as his security team.

As for Marissa and Tay... I'll let them tell you that story. Right now I need to get finished preparing for our launch party of the new studio.

TAY

"Don't mess around and get ate up." I teased Raven as she finished twisting the black twisty that disappeared into her dreads. She had it on so tight that she looked extremely surprised as her eyebrows lifted at the corners. Her golden eyeshadow complemented the dark berry lip stain she wore, and her burgundy bandage dress fit down her curves like it was custom made. I didn't really want niggas checking for my wife like that but, I was used to it. Yeah, you read that right. We have been officially married for a month, but because of how ratchet Marissa had been, I had kept it a secret.

"I will take it off if you don't want me to wear it," she stated, looking down at the 24 karat white gold bands that sat elegantly on her finger. I had the engagement ring custom made for her with a canary princess cut diamond because she loved the color yellow. It was surround by white baguettes that went all the way around, and her wedding band was a mixture of canary and white diamonds that went all the way around as well. Yeah, it set me back a bit, but it was worth it. Del had loaned me some of the money, thinking I was using it to repair my car.

"It's about time people find out. You ain't got to take nothing off, unless you wanna get out of this dress," I replied, kissing her neck.

"Don't you start being nasty. You know I get turned on easily," she warned.

"Let me make sure these kids ain't filthy."

I ran into the next room and Taviar and Tavonda were knocked out on the floor of her bedroom. *Dora the Explorer* was watching them as they slept peacefully. I knew they would be tired because we had kept them up all night so Raven could braid their hair. Tavonda had a head full of her like her mama, and it was halfway down her back already, so it took a while to get hers down. Taviar had some neat little braids with his name spelled out in them. Yeah, my wife got skills like that.

I had been keeping my hair cut low and waved out since I was the general manager of Motivations now. I figured I needed to look the part at all times since I would be going out and networking with artists and other performers. Since Raven cooked so well, I allowed her to provide the food for industry night which got her skills noticed enough for her to enroll in culinary school. We got us a nice little three bedroom in the suburbs, and even though it wasn't paid, for we treated it like it was.

"You grab one and I'll grab the other," I suggested as I scooped up Taviar.

My lil' man looked handsome in his burgundy button-down and black slacks. Starkisha had laughed at the loafers I bought him until she saw them on his feet. We all laughed at her as she made him pose for a million pictures. Tavonda had on a frilly little burgundy and white dress with a bow on the side. I thought the socks where a bit much because they covered half of her shoe, but Raven had insisted on making them. After we loaded the kids into the car I got the text message I had been dreading. Raven noticed my face and shook her head as I opened the door for her.

## MARISSA

Ain't no happy ending, at least not for me. While I was up in rehab recuperating and getting my life, a little bird told me that Tay had my baby around that Raven bitch. Now, his baby mama I could deal with because I knew she liked girls. But Raven was another story. I did a little background check and her nasty as used to be a stripper. Like really? That's what he went for? But he had the nerve to get on me about escorting.

He did bring my baby to see me every week, which was refreshing. I had not spoken too much about my ordeal with the police because I knew I could use it later. I know that Tay had something to do with Petey and Todd being killed. Their bodies were never found, but I remember being rescued by Tay. I had tried to get in touch with Sienna, who I found out had set my ass up, but it was like she fell off the earth. If Tay thought he would play hardball about a baby that wasn't his, then he was in for a treat.

When we finally were ordered to take a paternity test, I was excited. A bitch was on pins and needles. They would never let her go to a man that was not her father, and since nobody in Petey's family really knew the deal, I was all set. Even though Petey had signed the birth certificate, he apparently hadn't told too many people about it. Come to find out, that nigga had more kids than Mrs. Wayans. Imagine the shock I got when it was determined that Tay was the father. Baby, when I tell you I wanted another test done! The DNA specialist explained that baby can take on the characteristics of more than one man if the pregnant mother is sleeping around. I was too through.

The next thing we went through was determining who was a suitable parent. I didn't have a job and once I left rehab I had to move back in with Jason. I also didn't have a father figure to help me nor could I really get around without the use of a cane. I was fucked up. He had all his ducks in a row, even though I brought up his criminal record. They were able to determine he had a stable income as well as a nice home for her. I knew my sister and her husband had a hand in helping him with their bitch asses, but I had one last trick for those whores.

DELANO

Me, Pops, and Mr. Middleton posed for the camera as Pops held up his barbecue fork. He was wearing a striped apron that read, "Kiss me or kiss your ribs goodbye." Mr. Middleton looked like he had found the fountain of youth because his Blair Underwood looking ass was clean shaven and wore black Polo with matching black jeans and a pair of K.D's. I had never seen him so dressed down. Since I was in charge of grilling the seafood, I just wore a burgundy beater, with matching Akoo joggers and my black and burgundy Giuseppe sneakers. I let Mona talk me into wearing my hair down so I was looking quite Samoan at the moment. Before the end of the night I knew it would end up in my signature braid. My newest tattoo itched as the sun beamed down on it.

I found room on my left bicep to have a picture of Dannity tatted with her epitaph underneath. I thought Mona would give me grief, but she understood I had to honor the woman who had given me such a beautiful daughter. Speaking of which, I was surprised she wasn't attached to my hip. Having her here in the beginning was rough because she wanted to sleep with us every night, and then too, she missed her mama. I think what helped was getting her some counseling and allowing her to still see Lawrence so she could maintain some sense of normalcy.

"Well don't you look happy?"

I spun around and gave my mother a hug as she kissed both cheeks. I had to do a double-take. She wasn't in her signature black. I don't think I'd ever seen her in another color until now. She stood before me in a burgundy sundress that clung to her. Her hair was curled loosely and parted on the side, and she had on a faint touch of nude lipstick. Her eyes were lined in a dark color that wasn't quite black but it brought out the aqua blue in them. She looked beautiful.

"Don't stare too long. You may make your father jealous." She winked before walking over to where he stood talking. She slid her arms around his waist from the back and he pulled her in front of him. I wasn't ready to see all that, so I turned my head.

Tay and his family showed up and we had a few words before they went to get in line for plates. I could see Mona in the house playing with the kids. Mint Condition sang "Someone to Love," and couples began to abandon their plates to dance near the stage. I saw Tay grab Raven's hand as they left the kids sitting with Constantina. He had his arms firmly around her and the back of that dress stopped right above her voluptuous ass. I couldn't help but look, just like every other man in attendance. The sparkle of a wedding band caught my eye as he went to dip her.

It was like they were in their own world as everybody cleared out of the way to watch. I could see cell phones in the air everywhere as people recorded and took pictures of the beautiful moment. Once the song ended, they looked embarrassed to find everybody clapping for them. Raven hid her face in Tay's neck. He kissed her forehead before stepping up to the stage and whispering into Stokely Williams's ear. Stokely walked over and talked with the band briefly before handing the mic to Tay.

"Um how y'all doin'?" he said nervously. The crowd responded with a chorus of "okays and alrights before he continued. "As my boss can tell you, I don't like to talk in front of people. I am a performer and that's all I like doing, so without further delay, let me ask my beautiful wife to come up to the stage." Everybody clapped as he reached for Raven and she nervously joined him on stage.

"Awww hell naw! You married this bitch? Really? You turned a hoe into a housewife?" I was as mortified as everyone else when I turned to find Marissa making her way through the crowd.

I knew inviting her would be trouble, but Mona had insisted on it. She leaned on her cane slightly as she continued to walk up. The black dress she wore cut down the center of her breast and barely covered the front of her thighs while her hair was so big that it looked like a bad weave. She had tried to cover up the cuts on her face with makeup, but the shade was a bit too light, giving her a dead appearance.

"Get her the fuck outta!" I yelled.

Jason approached her, but she swatted at him. I knew it was on when I saw my mother-in-law walk up to her. I didn't even realize she had arrived. She looked flawless in her burgundy and gold wrap dress and matching suede pumps.

"You are embarrassing yourself. You need to come on."

Marissa snatched away from her mother, causing her drink to fall to the ground, and before Mr. Middleton could intervene, Marissa had swung on her mother, hitting her square in the jaw. A flurry of fists flew as security ran from every direction. Marissa's breasts were exposed as her cheap dress had all but been snatched off of her.

Mona-Lisa rushed my mother-in-law in the house and I was pissed off and embarrassed.

"Well that kinda went left field," Tay joked. The crowd laughed and the rest of the night went off without an issue. Tay and Raven sang some original pieces they had been working on, as well as *Breakin' My Heart,* which they covered with the band.

We had a nice ass time that night. I was sure that we would have many more memories to come as we eventually had plans on opening a soul food joint as well as a pole dancing studio. Yeah, it seemed like this hood love turned out to be a good love after all.


THE END

Made in the USA
Monee, IL
14 January 2021